Kingdom
Of The Curse

By: Kathy Roberts
Copyright 2017 Kathy Roberts

Cover Art by:
Author Laura Wright LaRoche
www.LLPIx.com or LLPix Designs.

Kingdoms of the Curse
by Kathy Roberts

Contact me with questions or orders any time at
kathyr121@live.com with one of my book titles in
the subject line so I know it's not spam.

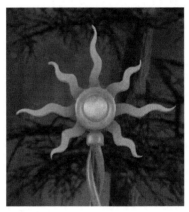

Copyright © 2017.   All rights reserved.

Cover Design by: Author Laura Wright LaRoche
Contact her at: www.LLPIx.com or LLPix Designs.

To my loyal fans.
I appreciate your continued support and am forever grateful for those who make it possible for me to continue writing. Without you, there would be no reason for me to write.

I absolutely love to write and to talk about my books.

I love to share my story and encourage other aspiring writers to continue with their journey and become the accomplished author they want to be.

For my daughter Breanna,
Don't ever give up on your dreams. Live in the moment, be ready for today. Always do right and work hard to make your dreams come true.

Thanks,
Kathy

I

I always want to thank God for what He is to me and for all He does for me.

I want to extend a very special thank you to my brother, Earl Sovine, and our friend, Joe Carpenter, for their creative inspiration, enthusium, and collaboration in making this book what it is.

Of course without my sister, Tammy Sovine, and my best friend Christie Edmunds, I would be working in the dark. They are amazing editors and chief among the gramatical policewomen. Their support is limitless!

Love you all!

1 - Cassandra

Cassandra stood at the edge of the forest. She was very careful to keep her toes behind the imaginary line that separated the yard and the woods. She looked as far as her eyes could see, yet saw nothing. She lifted her face to the sunshine and inhaled deeply. The smell was the forest. She could smell the moss, the wood, the stench of decay and animals. She smelled the slight fragrance of the flowers that bloomed near the edge of the forest where the sunshine was abundant. She could smell the faint scent of water, like there was a river or creek running through it. Maybe there was a beautiful waterfall somewhere hidden deep inside. She could imagine watching the water flow by while listening to all the chatter from the animals as they came to drink from the stream. Her senses were being bombarded with every scent imaginable, painting her a picture of a beautiful forest where everything was safe and gorgeous. Where the animals were so tame you could just walk up and pet one. She saw no danger, just beautiful scenery and pleasant thoughts and feelings.

She was being compelled to step into the woods, she knew she should turn and run as fast as she could back to the safety of her house, but yet she was not moving, not running away, not being scared; just standing there resisting but wanting to know more, wanting to see the things in there, wanting to understand what was happening and how it all affected her. She had surprisingly lifted her foot and had leaned a little toward the woods, like she was about to take a step; when she realized that she was no longer planted like one of the trees in the spot she'd claimed as her own. After finding herself stuck in it too many times to count over the years it seemed the natural place to be, but this realization brought her back to her senses and she quickly planted her foot back in its designated spot; the spot that had the undeniable imprint of her feet. There was a path worn in the grass all the way from the house to this spot. She couldn't remember how many times she had awakened in this spot. How many times she didn't even know how she'd gotten there and yet here she was again.

She had played this game before; knowing she would someday enter, but resisting, hoping and praying it would not be today. She felt the coolness of the forest calling to her, enticing her to step out of the hot sunshine that was scorching her skin and let the coolness envelope her and cool her body. Her hair lifted in the breeze begging to be unrestrained by the ponytail that held it fast—wanting to fly free in the wind and maybe flow out over the line, the line that currently held her captive. Her eyes darted around the trees, looking for signs of life; knowing there were animals and others in those woods, yet she saw no signs of any life at all. She felt her body swaying, like the leaves in the wind, straining to stay attached to the trees, yet leaning towards the edge—pulling at the restraints holding her there. She was careful not to let the tiniest part of herself pass over that line. She had felt the tug of something or someone for over six years, ever present in her life; urging her to come into the woods. She could hear her name being called in the whisper of the wind, even when there was no wind. She had chill bumps on her arms and down her neck onto her back. She knew something waited for her in those woods, but she had no clue who or what it might be. She found it strange that in all these years not one single time had she seen an animal of any kind or a person, or even a bird. It's like nothing was there, yet everything was there, just barely out of sight. Just across that line. If she'd only take that step, all would be revealed. She would be a part of it and it would be a part of her. She could come alive and be a part of this intriguing place.

She had grown up in that house beside those woods and had always known something evil lived there. Her mother had cautioned her on many occasions not to go into the woods and not to even play close to them. She wasn't to go by herself or with anyone else either. Her mother had made it seem like a life and death issue, so Cassandra had stayed away as best she could; but how could she control what happened in her sleep? She would wake up in that spot, not knowing how she'd gotten there. She often wondered what would happen to her if she hadn't awakened at the moment she did and had taken that step into the woods. Would she be lost forever? Would she be trapped there? Her mother never really explained it all to her, but the look in her eyes told Cassandra that there was danger there, as well as evil. Evil lived in those woods and it wanted to consume her. It was most of the time beyond her control that she'd come close to disobeying, but not because she'd wanted to. More times than not, she had awakened standing in this same spot, not knowing how she'd gotten there, or what woke her up. She'd heard her mother's voice calling her to come help her in those woods. Sometimes her mother was in sight near the house and she knew it couldn't have been her calling; yet it's what she heard. She'd heard children playing in there and so wanted a friend to play with. She'd heard laughter and music and she had desperately wanted to run in there and join the fun; but she had managed to stay out of the woods this long and she sure hoped she'd be able to stay away forever but the pull was getting stronger and came more often. It seemed to grow with every year she lived.

Drawing her to the final moment when she would enter and be engulfed with evil and either be consumed by it or destroyed by it. It sent chills down her spine just to think about it, yet it seemed like just walking right in there and seeing what was going on would be the most natural thing for her to do.

She was so torn, but she trusted her mother and knew she really should never be tempted above her resolve. She would never give in to whatever was taunting her and teasing her with the joy she had wanted for as long as she could remember. It was a lonely life being here away from all other people, just her and her mother. She didn't know why they lived by themselves. She didn't know what had happened to her father. Her mother would never talk about those things with any detail, she'd just say things like, he's gone, or there's evil in the woods, so don't go there. You don't want to end up like the others do you? Well she didn't want to end up like the others, but she did want to know about the others. Were she and her mother the only two people living on the earth, except for the evil in the woods? She had so many unanswered questions and her mother had so much fear. Why didn't they move away from the woods if that was the problem? Surely there were places the woods did not touch and couldn't reach? What had happened to all the other people and why had it not happened to them. She really wanted and maybe needed to know, but her mother was not willing to discuss anything about any of it. She just kept demanding Cassandra stay away from the woods.

She was so deep in thought about what things she didn't know about and the things she'd like to have and see in this life, that she didn't notice she was no longer alone. The sound of her name caused her to raise her head and look to see where the sound had come from. When she looked up, she saw a beautiful boy, about her age or size anyway, standing about fifty feet away, staring at her like he'd never seen a girl before and she found herself staring right back, knowing she'd never seen a boy before. Her mother had told her about them, but she'd never seen one or a girl either for that matter. She didn't know how he'd gotten there, just one second he was not and the next he was there. She leaned just a little to try to get a better look at him, when suddenly she heard her mother's voice calling her name. She sounded rather urgent and Cassandra turned to look back at her. She was running as fast as she could towards Cassandra. Cassandra knew something was wrong so she started running towards her. When they met, Cassandra was lifted up into her mother's arms and hugged tightly against her before she could even begin to ask what was wrong.

Her mother sat her down and turned her towards the woods. She looked intently for the little boy, but where he was standing she saw a very large wolf staring back at her. She was immediately admonished by her mother for being so close to the woods.

"I didn't go in mother. I was just looking at that boy. There was no wolf there before you came. You don't suppose he ate him do you?"

"No Cassandra, I don't think he ate that boy. I think he was that boy. There are many strange creatures in those woods that can entice you to enter and then harm you once you're there. He might eat you, or he might change you into a wolf and make you eat other children. There is evil and magic in those woods and I can't tell you enough times: Do NOT go into the woods."

Do you really think that wolf was a boy before?

I think it's time we had a real conversation about those woods and what lives there so you won't be going in there due to curiosity about it all. Come with me, it won't be long till dinner time and we'll talk about it then. I will answer any question you have and I'll tell you what I know about it all. You are twelve now and I think you're old enough to understand and learn about the real dangers that are living just a short distance from our house. They are waiting and watching us until just the right moment comes when they can get us, change us, devour us, or worse.

First of all, let's discuss the boy. He was the same as the wolf. Only a witch could see his boy form as when the curse was placed, he happened to be in his wolf form and he has to stay that way until the curse is lifted. He has no magic to change back and forth. They've all lost their magic. The fairies can no longer control the elements. There is much that is not taken care of and that's the reason the forest grows and continues to become black and evil. It was once a very beautiful place full of life, magic and color. The flowers no longer bloom like they did and light is minimal in there. The evil and dark magic has denied them and the beauty that once was Drenidore. They are surviving, but not really living. It's a cold damp place now that there is no love.

Thank you mama, I really do need to know because something in there keeps calling me and makes me come out here, even in my sleep. It wants me mama and I don't think I can keep resisting without some more information. I love you and I don't want to do bad or become something bad. Please help me any way you can mama. I'll listen and I'll be good, just don't keep stuff from me, so I can't be tricked. OK?

Of course darling, I won't keep anything from you and if it gets to be too much, just tell me and we'll wait a few days to talk more. I've wondered when this day would come. I think it's because you are so close to becoming a woman that the urge is stronger and the pull is so great. They want and need you to join them before you choose another path or come to the conclusion that none of it is real. Right now you have a great imagination and are open to many ideas, but the more you grow and mature, the less you'll believe in fairy tales, magic and stuff that go hand in hand with all that. I love you so much. I don't want anything to happen to my little girl—even if you're not going to be my little girl very much longer.

She smiled, took her mother's hand and they walked home to start dinner and have their talk.

She glanced back just once and saw the boy turning and walking slowly back deeper into the woods. He looked rather sad and she knew her mother would know why. She really wanted to talk to him, or any other person. She'd only ever known her mother. No friends or family were ever around, just the two of them. She also wondered about the one thing her mother said that seemed most important throughout all their conversation. They needed her. Who needed her, how many people or animals or demons lived in the woods? What could she do to help them, that they needed her so much? She was just a girl. She had no money and wasn't very strong. She had no clue what she could do to make her so valuable to whoever lived in the woods; but once again, her life was full of questions. Questions, she hoped she'd get answers to over dinner.

They lived in a small modest home and had land for a garden. There was nothing fancy about their house, but they had what they needed to survive. She would make their clothes, grow or catch most of their food and she did try to teach Cassandra the skills she would need to be a good wife someday. There were other skills she needed to start teaching her, but had been putting it off until the very last minute. She was afraid that minute had come and was dreading it due to the fact it might mean Cassandra would have to use those skills, yet exciting as she had so longed to share them with her and watch her blossom and become a stronger woman than she herself was.

They had lived in this house because Miranda was the first watch. She had been given the charge to monitor the growth of the forest and to make sure things didn't change in there. She was one of the princesses of the order of the good witches. She was protector of the queen and overseer to this side of the forest. She had held this position for six hundred and fifty years. When she moved into her home all those years ago, the forest was two miles away. Now it was about a thousand feet away. It was a slow progression, but it was growing and it would just be a matter of time before her house was consumed into the forest as well. Breaking the curse was the only way to stop it from consuming more and more of the country. She had spared her daughter long enough. They had to take action and begin her training.

What Cassandra was about to find out was her great imagination was no imagination at all, but an awareness of her surroundings, things, and people she'd seen in the woods and in her dreams. It was all real. All those things did exist and they all lived in her back yard. They started dinner and worked very well together, as usual. Cassandra set the table, made tea and the salad while her mother cooked some beef and vegetables, which would become soup for tomorrow's dinner. Cassandra loved to cook and was becoming good at it too. She was excellent at prep work, which is what she did the most of as her mother was a little too careful of her being near the fire.

They just chit-chatted while cooking and during dinner. After dinner was eaten and the dishes done; they sat on the couch, curled up together under a blanket so they'd be cozy and comfortable.

Miranda began to tell Cassandra the entire story of how the things that happened a few hundred years ago still affected them today.

Miranda laughed and said, here we go. Once upon a time. Cassandra laughed and said only fairy tales began that way mama. Miranda smiled and told her every fairy tale she'd ever heard was actually a true story and yet she'd started them all that way.

"You can't be serious! She cried, moving to look her mother directly in the eyes. All those stories you told me when I was little were true?"

Yes Dear, they were. Now on with my story, the greatest story ever to be told until we make a new one. One that will be the end all to this story. One that will make your name live forever and make you admired and revered by everyone; human, animal, or magical being.

2 - Zythora

It will be six hundred and fifty years this summer since it all began. Zythora was a young witch still in training and had made her first visit from the country into the town. She was in awe of the castle, the hustle and bustle of the people and all the sights and sounds of a busy township. There were all sorts of vendors at the marketplace and she was overwhelmed by it all, while being so thrilled and enthused by it all at the same time. She spent hours at the market, touching the silk fabric, smelling the foreign spices, admiring the jewelry, clothing and the musical instruments. The music captured her attention. The different sounds of the instruments seemed to help her mind drift off to foreign places and what she imagined had probably never entered into the minds of even the most serious traveler. After hours of being in the marketplace, she began to wander around the streets. She couldn't believe how different things were here. People of all colors, shapes, and sizes. Some spoke in different languages and some had thick accents that prevented her from understanding them even though they were speaking in her native tongue. She happened to come to the street in front of the castle and her heart leaped at the beauty of it. It was amazing and unlike anything she had ever seen. There were tall walls made of stone, some were rough and some were very smooth, almost like glass, they were so slick. Some of the corners were square and some were round with pointed tops. There were fancy colored flags atop those. It was a fortress, yet it seemed welcoming at the same time. She was wondering how beautiful it must be inside and how grand the décor must be. She envisioned the fireplaces that were so big a man could walk into them. She could almost see the staircases that would take several minutes to transcend, the chandeliers that would be swinging above everyone's head and would require a hundred candles to banish the darkness from the massive rooms. She knew that it would be drafty in places due to the size of it, but she also knew there would be warm and cozy places like the bedchamber with the heavily embroidered drapes around the sides to hold the heat in and the bed warmers would be so elaborate. Hers was iron, black and beginning to rust. The ones in the palace would have long wooden handles, smooth and had no splinters with a well-oiled shine. The pan itself would be made of brass, all shiny and beautiful to look at as it stood near the fireplace awaiting evening to fall so it could come to life with hot embers, ready to warm the bed of the king and queen, and of course all their visitors. Oh and the servants that would surely be required to run such a place and the personal maids to take care of any and every little detail she could imagine. She would be pampered beyond even her imagination. She could see herself living here very easily and decided she would do whatever it took to accomplish that goal. She was still standing there daydreaming an hour later, when a bunch of men on horseback came through the gate. They were dressed in all their finery and were just going for a ride. Zythora saw the most handsome man she'd ever seen in her life. He was very muscular, had dark wavy hair and deep blue eyes. He sat tall in the saddle and commanded the attention of everyone around him, just by his stature and presence. He wore the finest of riding gear with the family crest on his vest. He had a strong jawline and just looked like he was in charge of everything. His lips were full and he wore no facial hair. Then her eyes met the King's eyes and her heart began to flutter, her breathing became quick and she felt as she'd never felt before. She had instantly fallen in love. She didn't know what it was or even that love felt that way, but she was absolutely sure he was the most magnificent creature she'd ever seen. He did little more than let his eyes linger there a moment before urging his horse on. In seconds, he was gone. She turned to the guard and asked who that was. He thought she was touched in the head, but told her anyway, it was His Royal Highness, Lord Baltazaar, Ruler of Airamoor. And who is his queen, she asked. He again made a face but told her His Lordship had no queen as of yet. He'd just inherited the throne from his father who was thrown from his horse while hunting and dashed his head on a stone. The period of mourning had just ended, so he was sure the king would be in search of a wife very soon.

Zythora decided right then and there that she would be the next queen of Airamoor. She returned home and told her mother about all she had seen and witnessed in Airamoor. She explained that she would be the next queen. Her mother tried to bring her back down to earth a bit, but she was dead set on what she wanted and knew she could get it too. She sewed herself some fancy clothes with the help of her bewitched sewing needles, fixed her hair in the latest fashion, pinched her cheeks, cast a spell on the old broken down wagon and made herself a coach. She turned the two orphan boys who lived in a shack near her house, into the driver and footman and lastly, she turned the two geese they owned into horses. She waved her wand and the horses were hitched to the coach and were suddenly decorated with fancy hardware and feathers. She headed back to Airamoor in style to make the king fall in love with her.

On her way back to the city, she cast a spell on a local gentry who proceeded to give her a letter of introduction to the king as well as he gave her run of his home in the city. He gave her money and a maid to take with her. She had been in training quite a while as her mother had started early with her, so those were very easy spells for her and they didn't fade. She had to cancel the spell in order for them to return to their original places and looks. Some witches' spells would fade in a very short time, but she had grown strong in her short years. She practiced every day since she was five years old. She'd practiced on the animals and creatures that lived in or near her home. She'd conjured many things from nothing anyone could see and she could even braid her hair without ever touching it. She had many talents and great focus to direct her magic just where she wanted it.

Once she'd taken up residence in the borrowed home, she wasted no time sending a messenger to the king telling of her arrival and asked if she might visit sometime to extend her benefactor's regards to the king and to express her desire to be of service to him as well.

Now the king thought himself quite the ladies' man and the letter she'd sent gave her all the recommendation he needed to convince him to entertain her. Who knew, she just might strike his fancy.
He arranged a dinner in two days and she was

invited along with nine other couples from the families of select noblemen in his kingdom. They were all young adults and they enjoyed a wonderful time, the food was exquisite, there were musicians who played beautifully and the dancing was heavenly. She'd never had such a good time in all her life. The king was quite taken with her, of course the charm she used on him helped that along quite a bit. She didn't trust her own natural charm, but felt she needed to seal the deal with magic. No one knew who she was or what she was and a sprinkle of magic around the room and on all the guests made them all believe she just might make a good queen for their king. She loved all the delicacies and the attention he paid her. He would lay his hand on hers or touch her arm and even when they danced his hand would be at the small of her back. She didn't know if this was scandalous or not, she just knew she liked it and as she was becoming a woman, her body responded with feelings she never knew existed. She wanted this to continue. She wanted this to be how she spent the rest of her life. Beautiful, happy, full of life, good food and romance.

Their romance, or should we say charmance was stellar and had developed at an incredible rate. They'd had party after party and she was on his arm at every state dinner, party or meeting even. Had a stranger come into town, they would have assumed she were already the queen. They were rarely seen one without the other and Zythora loved all the attention and the king wasn't too bad to look at either. Zythora had a slight build, but was very strong. Her hair would make a raven envious, but her eyes were black and quite uncommon. They were beautiful when she smiled, but they were ominous when she frowned. They did make a handsome couple.

She'd set her sights high and nothing was going to get in her way. Nothing progressed in his treatment of her, but he never stopped his attentiveness either. This had been going on for a little over six months and she felt very secure in her position. Many women had passed through his life during that time, but she was the one on his arm and it didn't bother her one little bit that her magic was what kept him there. She didn't care what the king wanted or what mattered to him. This was all about her and always would be. She'd see that he was happy, but he probably would never know real happiness as he was living under her spell. She was well on her way to getting just what she wanted and magic was a part of who she was, so using it was very natural to her.

She had gone home for two days to collect her mother, a few personal belongings and to close the house. She needed further training as she had not completed her lessons so she decided she'd bring her mother to her new home and she could continue learning and practicing there. The entire journey would only take her four days. It wouldn't be too long until they both would move into the palace. It had, after all, been six months since their first meeting and that was long enough to wait. If he didn't ask her in the next fortnight, she was going to cast a spell on him compelling him to ask for her hand in marriage. She was not going to fool around with this one. She was going to rule this kingdom and he would be her puppet. She smiled every time she thought about that. How wonderful to have a whole kingdom to rule. Everyone would have to bow down to her. She wasn't sure what she would do with all her power yet, but she knew whatever she wanted, the people would do. One way or another.

Zythora knew what she wanted and the power she had with her magic, along with the power she would control in being the queen, would make her unstoppable in anything she desired. She was almost floating home. She had everything figured out and knew the rest of her life would be charmed and she'd have no worries at all. She was ecstatic with herself and her new life. Nothing could stop her now!

3 – Angelica

When Zythora left for home, King Baltazaar
arranged a hunting party with his friends. They
headed into the forest to secure a stag for the
upcoming feast and any other small game they
might find along the way. He loved to hunt
and the forest was his favorite spot. He would
bird hunt in the fields, but the forest seemed
magical to him. Little did he know at the time,
but it was filled with magic, very real magic, not
just the illusion people perceived when
something was so special. They were riding
along as quietly as they could and watching for
game. The forest was dense and they had to
be careful that the trees didn't snag their bow
right out of their hands, like a person trying to
stop them from pursuing the game.

They happened upon a magnificent stag and
chased him deeper into the woods. When the
king and his guard were separated from the
rest of the hunting crew, the stag turned and
charged at them before they could draw their
bows to shoot, he would have easily been able
to run them through with his massive antlers; yet
he stopped inches from the king and stood
looking him in the eye, waiting. The king was
breathless but dared not move as the stag was
too close for comfort and could still gore him
with one swift turn of his head. When the
tension seemed thick enough to cut, a

beautiful woman walked out from behind a tree and came right up to the stag, patted him on the neck, tiptoed and whispered in his ear and he turned toward her and seemed to relax. She then turned toward the king, curtseyed and introduced herself.

She explained she was the queen of the fairies and they lived deep in this forest with the animals. They were all friends and this particular stag was one of her best friends, and his name was Conrad. When she had need of protection, he was always at her side and she would be most grateful if the king would give up his plans of having him for dinner. She told Baltazaar that she'd already told Conrad that he would be safe today and should relax. If the king were still inclined to kill someone, she would offer herself instead.

Baltazaar sat high in his saddle watching every move she made. She was so delicate, yet seemed strong physically and mentally. She would be a challenge to outwit he was sure; and she was so charming as well. She must have been born with grace and elegance as it exuded from every pore. She seemed to float over the roots and fallen branches that lay before her path. She truly was a queen in every sense of the word. She was beautiful and possessed a kindness and charm that melted his heart. He was sure his heart actually grew a little bigger just for having met her. He acknowledged to himself that he loved this woman and would do everything in his power to make her his queen, not just the fairy queen. He knew she would make him a better man, and most definitely a better king.

He quickly dismounted and bowed low while sweeping his hat from his head and making a great production of swishing it through the air to rest behind his back, and then he reached for her hand. She extended it and he gently took her delicate hand in his and kissed it ever so gallantly. He introduced himself and then spoke to the stag, apologizing for scaring him and assured Conrad that he now understood his place as King in these woods and he would be safe as long as he, Baltazaar, was king of Airamoor. He then turned back to the beautiful woman and asked if he might know her name, so that when he told of her beauty, kindness, and elegance; he would have a name to go with his praise.

She looked into his eyes and smiled. "My name is Angelica." He stared deeply into her green eyes, he'd never seen eyes this color, but he had seen that look before. He saw into her heart when she looked at him this way. He believed at that moment that she might just love him too. How did this happen so fast? Were they destined to find one another? Were they married in a past life? He didn't know and he didn't care; he had met her now and he knew just how much he wanted this woman by his side for the rest of his life and he fully intended to make it happen. He realized he was still staring and hadn't said a word to her, she must think him daft.

"Uh, excuse me, I'm so sorry. I didn't mean to stare, but I'm just taken off guard with you. I have yet to meet a woman as complete as you are Queen Angelica. That is a most appropriate name, for surely you have come from heaven to grace this world and my life with your presence. You are not only beautiful, elegant and kind, but I believe you are revered by all who know you. I perceive you are an excellent judge of character, a good friend, and a protective and fair ruler. I would count it my honor and privilege to show my hospitality in inviting you to dinner at my palace. I would like to get to know you and hear all about your kingdom. I never knew fairies were real. I'd heard tales of fairy folk, but I thought you were just stories people made up to entertain their children and teach them to be good and kind as well as to spark their imaginations to believe all things were possible and we should all be more like fairies as they possessed some of the greatest qualities of all creatures. I'm glad to have been here today to witness this encounter and for the honor of speaking with a great ruler such as yourself. Maybe you would be so kind as to show me your kingdom since I am so close and I would be overjoyed to meet your family as well. I think we can make a treaty to protect your kingdom and homes as well as your friends who live here in this magical forest."

Angelica was intrigued by Baltazaar and she also wanted to see what was outside her kingdom, plus the prospect of him ordering protection for them all was too worthwhile not to share some time with him. She had noticed that he was fit and more handsome than any male she'd had the pleasure to look upon. Yes, he was quite nice to look at. When she raised her eyes again to meet his to answer, her heart skipped a beat when she saw the look in his eyes. His deep blue eyes shone brightly with a light she'd seen in her father's eyes when he had looked at her mother. She realized she was in love with this man. How could that be? She'd never heard of love coming so quickly and lasting so long. This was a strange feeling she had and she knew it wasn't fake, but emanating from deep within her being. She didn't want to rush into anything, but she really didn't want to watch him leave either. "Of course, I'll show you my home and introduce you to my closest friends and family. I would also be delighted to join you at your home for dinner soon."

Wonderful! He exclaimed. Shall we go? Would you care to ride with me or do you have a mount tied somewhere close? She smiled and said she'd ride with him if that were amenable with him. He swiftly mounted his horse, scooted back on the saddle and then reached down to take her hand and lift her up in front of himself and into his saddle. She was light as a feather. He reached around her to gather the reins and his heart soared when she put her hands on his and leaned back into his embrace and indicated she was ready to go and that he should proceed west.

They were very close to the heart of the forest, so it was a short walk for the horses and when they arrived, she truly didn't want to move from within his arms to dismount. He was strong and muscled, yet very delicate in the way he handled her. He swung his leg over the horse, dismounted and reached up to lift her down. He slid her down right in front of him, very close, she looked up and their eyes met. He held her around the waist and her hands were on his upper arms as she'd left them there after he sat her down. They just stood looking into each other's eyes; oblivious of everyone and anything else around them. It was a full two minutes before they realized there was a crowd gathering. They both dropped their hands and she began to point out her kingdom. All the houses were in the trees, most were small but in the center of it all was a grand palace where she lived. It was in a great tree that stood taller than all the others, and it expanded to other trees on the sides so as to command attention and honor among all onlookers. Many of the smaller houses were connected by swinging bridges draped ever so perfectly around the entire complex, like decorations on a tree. Angelica heard someone clear their throat and the magic was broken. She looked and saw her brother waiting for an explanation for this human she'd brought into their world. She introduced them and told Hunter they had been invited to dinner. His immediate response was hmpf. She gave him the look and he immediately made their guest welcome and smiled while doing so. When Angelica turned back to join in the conversation, Hunter got the full effect of their affection for each other. He was pretty sure he might be losing a sister and gaining a kingdom. He really didn't want to rule, but if it made his sister happy, he'd gladly do whatever was required.

She showed Baltazaar around and explained their sections and classes of fairies. They had different jobs and they controlled the elements, so depending on their talents, they might make flowers grow or cause the river to flow. The water fairies could bend water and make it flow a different direction than it had before, thus changing the river or moving it sideways to avoid a flood. They were very talented. There was so much to see, touch and learn, he was like a kid in a candy store. The more he saw and learned, the more he wanted to know and see. Some fairies were very small and lived in toadstools, they had nothing wrong with them that they were so small, it was just how they were. They were the ones who flew the most. All fairies could fly, but many weren't going far enough to need to use their wings, so they just walked. Some thought it a shame not to use their beautiful delicate wings as they were a special gift given only to fairies, but others felt like they were showing off when they flew around. Most of the younger ones were the fast flyers. Young people were always in a big hurry it seemed.

All the fairies were smaller as a whole than humans, but they were not tiny by any means, except for the one group of toadstool fairies. Some were tall and some were very rotund. Just on average probably 6 inches shorter than the average human. He found Angelica to be about eight inches shorter than his height, but he was a couple inches taller than most. They wouldn't be a matched couple in that regard, but they would be a stunning combination of tall and regal accompanied by delicate and commanding in her own right. He checked to see if they all had green eyes and they didn't. They were pretty much run of the mill people who were just a little smaller than most humans and possessed wings. But the part he loved was their appreciation of the elements and their dedication to their jobs taking care of it all.

She introduced him to a few of the trolls. They were a grumpy lot who lived under the bridges and big tree roots. They were protective of their land and didn't like being disturbed. They sometimes grew pretty large and normally were ugly by human standards. They were very strong and they took care of the land, planting trees and shrubs; protecting it all from those who would cut down the trees or plow it up.

He met the gnomes who wandered around the forest. They were travelers. They looked like old humans, but were very small, usually only two to three feet tall. They could cast spells and would turn to stone to camouflage themselves from predators. They were gardeners by trade, so they took care of the plants and flowers gracing the forest floor. They kept to themselves pretty much, but were talkative if truly engaged.

She showed him the changelings or shape shifters as many people called them. Their prince was a grizzly bear. They shifted from human to animal form depending on the need for survival. If they were threatened in one form they'd shift to the other. There was no rhyme or reason for which form they preferred, it usually depended on the situation or the individual. Some just preferred to stay in their animal form over their human. They were gentle in either form unless threatened, then they were ferocious.

The last group for him to meet was the imps. They were in essence, fairies, but they were small in size and were considered tricksters. Some were considered tools of the devil as they were often familiars of a witch or warlock. They were mischievous troublemakers. They were sometimes really mean in what they did, but most meant no real harm. Generally, they were avoided by most and kept to themselves unless they crossed paths with another being, no matter who or what it was.

Baltazaar was intrigued with all the diversity of this world and yet how they all got along and respected the leadership and authority of Angelica. He'd never imagined they all existed, much less the fact he was in love with one of these woodland creatures.

Baltazaar and Angelica became engaged and if you saw one, you probably saw the other. He had forgotten all about Zythora. He had enjoyed her company, but she had not had the effect on him that Angelica did. He didn't love Zythora, he just liked her and when

Angelica was around, he never gave anyone else a second thought. He liked being in love. It was like sunshine and cake every day.

Zythora sent a letter to the palace letting him know she'd returned and wanted to see him and introduce him to her family. He didn't respond. She hadn't seen them together yet, so she thought possibly he was ill, so she sent another letter. This time the courier came back and told her about the couple and said she might not receive a reply at all as the king was very smitten; but he'd left it with the guard just in case. Needless to say, Zythora felt betrayed and hurt. She loved Baltazaar. She was only gone four days and he'd cast her aside for some green eyed petite woman with long blonde hair. She wasn't prettier than Zythora, but she had an appeal that drew men and women alike to her. She connected with people and was genuine and honest. She smiled and was concerned about their needs. She probably would make a better queen, but Zythora wasn't going to have it. Not without having her say and destroying whatever she could of them. She'd been scorned and that was unacceptable.

She decided she'd give him a month to come back to her. Men were simple and could be easily swayed by a pretty face and a sprinkle of magic wouldn't hurt either. She would plot her revenge during that time, so she'd be ready should he decide to stay with his second choice. She didn't have to wait long, just before the month was up the decree was announced that they'd be married on the last day of the month.

Zythora was livid; she consulted with her mother and made plans to destroy them both. No! All! She vowed the minute they were wed; she'd curse all humans in the kingdom. Then she'd curse all animals in the forest. Next, she'd curse all the creatures (fairies, trolls, changelings, gnomes, and imps) in the woods. Then she'd curse Airamoor and put it to sleep so no one would ever be happy there again. It wasn't a sleep like the body does when it's tired, but a sleep of the mind and soul. Not caring about what's going on with their lives or anything around them. The kingdom in all its glory would die and lay in ruins while the occupants lived forever in a state of discord and lack of emotion, awaiting someone to undo the curse. The curse that would never be undone. After that, she'd curse love. Anyone entering what was left of Airamoor or who entered the forest would not be able to love. She lost her happiness, so she would not let love thrive. Lastly, she would curse the land so that the forest would increase and the outlying lands would decrease until the magic had consumed the entire kingdom of Airamoor into the forest.

She would reign until the end of time and her magic would grow with the forest until she became the strongest witch in the world. This would make people sit up and take notice of her. She would be supreme on this planet and have and do whatever she wanted.

She could have anything and never be concerned with Baltazaar, or anyone else she didn't want to see or hear about. She would never see their faces again and that pleased her very much.

4 – The Wedding

The day came and Angelica was stunning in all her glory. She wore a gown so white it actually gave off a glow. Well maybe it was the fairy magic but it glowed none-the-less. She was glowing herself and so happy to be marrying her love, Baltazaar. Her brother Hunter walked her down the aisle to her groom who was quite breathtaking himself in his white uniform with gold trim and buttons. The ladies mourned losing their chance at becoming a queen, but they could tell this union would be good for their country. His blue eyes shone with love as they found the green eyes of his betrothed walking toward him down the aisle. The cathedral wasn't big enough to hold everyone so closest and highest ranking were inside and the rest of both kingdoms waited on the outside straining to hear any snippet of the ceremony. Both Baltazaar and Angelica had walked from the edge of the crowd outside all the way into the cathedral so everyone could have a look at the happy couple.

Zythora was there, front and center near the entrance to the cathedral. Neither of them glanced her way. She was nothing to them and that fueled her anger even more. When they were pronounced husband and wife and the cheers were finished. The happy couple turned to walk back down the aisle and lightning struck in front of them and all around the inside and outside of the cathedral. People ran for cover not knowing what was happening. Zythora walked across to the top step so she could be seen by everyone inside and out. She raised her arms and began to speak. Her voice was amplified by her magic and there wasn't a soul who didn't hear her decree.

"This day is proof that I have been scorned. Baltazaar made promises to me and he has shamed and dishonored me here today." He shouted his denial of any promises, but she kept talking. "I will this day deliver curses upon all humans, the animals and other creatures in the forest, on Airamoor, love itself and the land containing both your kingdoms. Airamoor and Drenidore will both be destroyed and love will never be allowed in all this land. Forever!" She cast her first spell on Baltazaar and Angelica. She reached her arms toward the heavens and lightening continued to strike all around. The sky became dark, but there was a glow around her as her magic could be seen, emanating from within her and rippling out in all directions. She cried in a thunderous voice her curse…

"My rage grows high as the flame of my love burns low. Let this couple, Baltazaar and Angelica, who dare'ith to keep my love from me, feel love no more for each other. Let them

now be apart and never again as one. May every human dwelling in Airamoor be the same. Stuck in their existence; never aging, living, but never again to feel love of any kind. Loveless souls, seeking and never knowing what they're searching for. Gods, Goddesses, and Spirits of love this is what I call upon thee to do: Break their hearts and let them be eternally apart. Do this for me. So Mote It Be. I command this spell to be in place for as long as I live upon this earth."

Baltazaar and Angelica took one last look at each other and they both were whisked away with the wind, her to her forest and him to his castle. At this event, everyone took off running to their homes or any shelter they could find. They did not want to be involved in any more of Zythora's curses and it was probably what saved many of them.

Now to curse the animals she screamed.

"My rage and hatred continues to abound and now I curse all animals living in or on the ground. Inside the forest you will stay. I curse the birds who fly in the sky that any that leave the boundaries of the forest shall die! Gods, Goddesses, and spirits of the earth, this is what I call upon thee to do. Trap them there that they may never be free. Do this for me. So Mote It

Be. Again, I command this spell to be in place for as long as I live upon this earth."

Any animal or bird inside the forest could never leave, what she didn't count on, however was the few who were not back inside the boundaries of the forest when the curse was spoken. They would be free, but could not enter the forest or they would be trapped by the curse as well. It was a very sad day for that part of the earth wherein all those dwelt.

Her anger and hatred had doubled by the time she had spoken the second curse and she was not finished. Her heart was consumed by hate, vengeance, and malice. Her soul was black as night and she had little hope of changing for the better.

You creatures of the forest who live and breathe, talk, and make plans, you are not exempt from my wrath. I have more hatred for you as you are the cause of my agony.

My rage has tripled against you this day. You bore the abomination that stole my love away. You knew and you did nothing. You showed joy at the union and cared not that I suffered so.

"I call upon the Gods and Goddesses, and the animal spirits and magic; wipe out the magic

from Drenidore and the surrounding forest. May all inside those boundaries lose their powers and the favors given them by the Gods! Do this for me. So Mote It Be. I command this curse to be in place for as long as I live upon this earth."

Three curses have I placed on those of you within the sound of my voice. Three curses more have I to place. Drenidore has received her curse, now Airamoor shall meet her fate!

"My fury is growing like a fire with too much to consume. The flames of my wrath lick out to all I see, touch and feel. I will be avenged for this betrayal. I call upon the Gods, Goddesses and the earthly powers that create kingdoms for mortal men and women. I curse you Airamoor that there will be no joy or happiness within the walls of the palace for as long as I live upon this earth. Do this for me. So Mote It Be."

My pain and agony cannot be measured. I have been denied the one thing I wanted most. It was stolen from me. I felt the love for Baltazaar, but now I only feel hatred and betrayal. If I cannot feel love, I will not suffice there to be love for anyone.

"I call upon the Gods and Goddesses of Love, strike this emotion from the people, creatures, and animals that live behind these palace walls

and inside the boundaries of Drenidore. Do this for me. So Mote It Be. I command this spell to be in place for as long as I live upon this earth."

The wind and lightening had not abated, but had grown stronger with each curse. Zythora was a mad woman by the time she was ready to issue the sixth curse. Her countenance was distorted. She was pure evil spouting her curses.

"I call upon the Gods and Goddesses and nature itself to fulfill this curse. I proclaim Drenidore shall begin to consume Airamoor and Airamoor will no longer be a thriving kingdom, but vanquished inside a dark enchanted forest that has lost its magic. All will fear to enter Drenidore as it will take their magic and never let them leave. Do this for me. So Mote It Be. I command this spell to be in place for as long as I live upon this earth."

When Zythora had finished speaking, she was spent, exhausted and weak. She had no energy left as she'd used it all to curse everything and everyone; or so she'd thought. Airamoor and Drenidore had friends who were not affected by the curse as they were outside the boundaries of the forest and not behind the palace walls. Zythora had let her emotions overwhelm her. Her rage had consumed her and her curses were not as encompassing as she had thought. During all the thundering and lightening Zythora had created, the band of White Witches, those who only worked good magic, were gathering and devising their own plan. They would curse Zythora and stop her reign of terror while they worked to find a way to remove or fulfill the curses. She had gained so much power they knew they could not kill her, not now, but she would be weakened after using so much magic and they could control her while they worked to change everything.

As soon as Zythora collapsed, having spent all her magic, before she had a chance to rest and recharge, the band of White Witches made their move.

5 – White Witches

Lorissa began to speak and they all joined hands. "Chant sisters, chant for the powers of goodness to overcome the powers of darkness while I speak the spell. So they began to chant:
Powers that be, give us the power
Powers of light, expel the darkness
Powers that be, give us the power
Powers of light, expel the darkness.

As they chanted over and over in unison, they could feel the charge of power surge through them. They felt the energy flow to Lorissa from each of their bodies. They kept chanting this until after the time Lorissa spoke her spell. They were as one. The air was so charged with their energy, that Lorissa was lifted off the ground a few feet, her hair was loosened from the wind swirling around the group and her gown floated on and flapped in the wind so much it looked as if she were dancing. There was a definite buzz of energy in the air, it was getting so loud, they could barely hear Lorissa's curse being spoken. No one looked towards Zythora as the chain of power would have been broken, they merely trusted she was captive by the powers of good and light and they would be able to complete the curse against her and hopefully manage to save the kingdoms sooner than later.

"I call upon the Gods and Goddesses to give me strength and power to overcome this wicked evil witch who has wrought so much evil this day. Give us the power to defeat her. I command that Zythora be bound in a box, buried in the center of Drenidore, until we find a way and break the curses she has decreed this day! I command she have no power to do any more harm. Do this for me. So Mote It Be. I command this spell to be in place for as long as I live upon this earth or until we find a way to kill Zythora and release everyone from the curses she has uttered this day."

Once Lorissa's spell had been spoken, the energy started to dissipate and she slowly descended back to the earth. They all turned to look at Zythora. There was lumber circling above her and once all the power they'd felt had moved to where Zythora was, the lumber became a box and Zythora was lifted and placed inside. Chains were wrapped around the box on all sides and a seal was placed on it. Then it flew through the air into the forest. They knew it was in the heart of Drenidore, and buried like their curse commanded. It would take some powerful magic to break her free of this, but the white witches wasted no time in getting home to research and find a way to fix all this and bring their kingdoms back. They didn't want anyone with evil magic to find her and they didn't want her to recharge and regain enough power to get out by herself.

Cassandra had sat wide-eyed during the entire story and it had gotten very late as it was a long story to be told. She finally looked at her mother and exclaimed. Wow! She had no other words and none were going to form right now either. It was incredible to think all this happened so long ago and no one had been able to break the curse and that Zythora was still in those woods. Finally she spoke. So all this is true. There are witches and all those other creatures you talked about.

Yes child it's all true, no fairytales here tonight.

"Do you think she's who's calling to me from the forest mama?

I think she might be and that worries me a little. If she's pulling at you, then her strength is returning and that's not good for anyone.

It's very late child, let's continue this in the morning. We need to get some sleep. Why don't you sleep in my bed tonight, this has been a lot for you to take in and I don't want you having nightmares.

Ok mama. But you're saying there's more? More of her wickedness, more of the story?

Yes there is and I'll tell you all about it in the morning after breakfast. We need to get it all in the open and I'll answer any questions you have when I'm done.

So they got ready for bed and snuggled against each other to dispel the chills and any evil lurking near them.

It was a while before Cassandra could go to sleep, she was thinking about the story and the fact it was all real. She worried a little about Zythora coming to get her, but then she remembered her mama would always be there to protect her, so she felt better about it all and finally drifted off to sleep.

6 - The Rules

It was morning and past their usual breakfast time. They had slept longer than anticipated due to being up so late the night before. Miranda woke first and got Cassandra up so they could begin their day.

They worked together getting breakfast ready so they could talk about the rest of this story when they'd eaten. Breakfast was very good, the house was filled with the smell of bacon. It was both their favorite food for any time of the day, not just breakfast, and they were both starving—probably more so due to the aroma of the bacon. Telling and hearing the story was draining for them. It involved a lot of energy and they felt the drain, but they were rested now and would go on with a more pleasant day.

OK mama, let's get on with this story.

Well, Miranda began, since you're so anxious, the white witches uncovered some things in their research on how to break spells and how to reverse spells, even on how to turn a spell against the original speaker of the spell. The main things they discovered were these.

Rule 1. The only person who could break the spell had to be Zythora herself or be in the

<u>direct bloodline with her.</u>

Do we know who is in the bloodline mama?

We do. There is a record kept of all witches.
Actually, we are in Zythora's bloodline,
Cassandra.

We are witches? She asked wide-eyed again.

Yes dear, we are. You've just not been
exposed to any witchcraft or learned your
trade yet. That time is upon us and I'll have to
begin your training very soon.

I have magic in me? That's so cool! Wait, so
we could break the curse!

It's not quite that easy. We could if we meet all
the requirements and are strong enough in our
magic, but you are still a child and untrained,
so you would not have enough strength in
yourself to do it

But with a lot of witches to chant for me to
have the power, then I could, right?

That would help considerably my child, but
Zythora is very powerful so we'd have to have a
lot of help.

Wait I'm sorry to keep interrupting mama, but

things are beginning to click and I'm seeing the whole picture. I'm a witch! You said only a witch could see their true form; so that's why I could see that little boy in his wolf form and his human form?

That's absolutely correct. You've already seen evidence of your powers as a witch. Once we begin your training you'll find you have a lot of power and will be gaining more as we progress.

Rule 2. The witch has to carry the name of an angel.

Before you ask, yes you do. Way back, all those years ago, when we discovered that was one of the requirements, all good witches began naming our children after angels as we didn't want a technicality to keep us from accomplishing our goal of destroying Zythora in the event one of us had the call, knowledge, the will, the power, and met the requirements.

So you are named after an angel too then? She smiled.

Yes I am; but not because of the curse. I was already grown when Zythora uttered her curses. I am her cousin, her mother and mine are sisters. I'm also very proud of my name as it means I am one of the few who use my power for good and never for evil. No matter what happens.

You were already grown then?! So you are over six hundred and fifty years old?! I can't believe it mama, how can that be?

I'm a witch darling. We live very long lives due to the magic in us. I am a princess of the order of the white witches and I was placed as first watch to this side of the forest. I've been watching its progression for all these years and monitoring anything unusual and reporting it back to Queen Lorissa. I am actually almost seven hundred years old. Witches can easily live a couple thousand years or more if they are careful how they use their magic. Zythora spent a lot of magic in her revenge. She probably lost about five hundred years of her life span that day between using her energy and being placed in Drenidore where magic has been removed. Unlike the other creatures, she can regain some power, but not enough to break the spell holding her there so the lack of power has robbed her of some of those years as well.

Rule 3. The witch has to be willing to do it. She can't be forced.

Why would she have to be forced? I think it would be the best thing ever to be able to help so many people get back to their lives and be freed from the fear and anxiety of the curses.

Well not everyone considers it an honor Cassandra, some feel it would be a curse itself. A job bigger than they could handle. They are afraid to combat such a powerful witch. They don't believe in themselves enough and they don't believe the higher powers would help them. They feel unworthy and don't want to assume the risks to themselves. They could actually die in a battle this strong. One thing they haven't thought about though is during the beginning Zythora will still be weaker than normal, so they would have that additional advantage.

Rule 4. They have to believe above everything else that they are the chosen one to do it.

Should a witch attempt to break the curse and destroy Zythora, and she had any doubts, it would kill her. Some have thought they were chosen over the years, but most are afraid to try it—they have doubts and with doubts in this case, comes death. The person has to be as strong or stronger than Zythora in order to defeat her and a lot of that comes from within, not just what they've learned to do as a witch or what they've already accomplished in their lives. They have to feel that call for a duty beyond what is required of them.

<u>And Rule 5. The counter spell has to be spoken
on their 16th birthday.</u>

This is another reason many of them chose not
to try. They were young and had little
experience so they didn't believe they could
do it and didn't want to risk their lives.

Witches come into a great amount of power on
their 16th birthday, it's a rite of passage. You
can do a lot of things before then and you can
cast many spells that are binding, but that day
you will be more powerful than any other day in
your life. I'll teach you all you need to know for
this cause as well as your responsibilities and
needs for the rest of your life. I believe you
have felt this call because you are nearing that
birthday and have limited years to learn, train,
and perfect your talents and skills.

When can we start my training mama? I
believe I am the chosen one and we need to
get busy. Don't look at me that way. Why else
would Zythora try to get me into those woods?
She knows somehow that I'm the one and she's
trying to get me before I can get her.

You may be right my love, but I'm not sure we
can risk it. I'm not sure I want to risk losing you.

I know you believe in me mama. I also know if
she is freed we will be dead anyway as she will

take revenge on all responsible for trapping her in that box all these years. I'd rather go out fighting to save everyone than be defeated before I ever began. That's why we have to start my training, you'll see. I'll show you and it will become evident to you and any other witches that this is the time. Our people, animals and creatures have been captive for too long. I know it's me mama and you've got what it takes to train me in everything I need to know to do it. Plus you'll be right by my side for it all. It's me. It truly is and I think you know it too.

Miranda nodded her head and looked straight into Cassandra's eyes and spoke the hardest words of her entire life. "I DO think you are THE One. I do believe you can defeat her and restore these kingdoms and I do believe I can help you learn what you need to know in order to accomplish this monumental task. I just don't want to take the chance of losing you should you have a stray thought.

I won't mama. I know I am the one. I know with you by my side, I can do this. I know we can gather more white witches together to chant and boost our strength. I know we can bring these kingdoms back to where they used to be and restore true love in our part of the world. Don't be afraid, mama, I'm not. I'll be strong and you can be too. We can do this.

Now let's get started. These people need freed and Zythora needs to be destroyed. We need freed as well. We owe this to ourselves as much as everyone else.

Well hold your horses there girl. We have to clean up this kitchen and then we'll get started.

Couldn't you just this once use magic to clean the dishes?

Well I could, but that won't teach you discipline in housekeeping.

No, but it will teach me that some things are more important and the lives involved in these curses are much more important than dishes. I really want to learn mama and I'll work hard too. I want her out of my head. I want a normal life and not live in fear of some agitated woman who's stressing because she lost a man she never really had. She'd used magic to make him love her. How in the world did she think that would work? Or did she not care if he loved her later, after she got the kingdom? I don't understand greed and jealousy at all.

I'll explain it to you darling and we'll definitely get started on your training, but the dishes come first and patience is a virtue so doing the dishes first, will help you learn patience and discipline. You're going to need them both along with that fierce go get them attitude you just displayed. You can't just jump into some things, you have to always be careful as there is much danger linked hand in hand with magic. It can sometimes be more dangerous for the witch casting a spell than for the intended one receiving the curse.

How about you teach me the spell for cleaning the kitchen with magic? I have to start small and that sure seems like a good plan to me. Learn magic and clean the kitchen at the same time.

You are impossible, but again, you're right. Here's what you do. Imagine what you want done, then see it happening. Don't lose concentration or you'll break a dish, or drop something and make a mess. They laughed the entire time they "cleaned" which consisted of less than a minute and that was for the entire house, not just the dishes or kitchen.

Very good darling. That was some very nice concentration. You're going to be a very fast learner for sure.

7 - Javan

At the edge of the forest of Drenidore stands a young grey wolf, listening with his keen ear, trying not to miss a single word that Miranda was speaking to Cassandra. He was never told the story about how and why it happened and he definitely never knew there was a chance of changing their fate. He was tired of being trapped in this forest. Not being able to run free and explore the countryside. He longed for fresh air and sunshine. He could feel the forest closing in and suffocating the lives inside it. Turning darker every day he lived. He longed to walk on his two feet again. He wanted to be the boy sometimes. He enjoyed playing with the fairies, but many of them feared him in his animal state. Even though Drenidore had gained square footage every year for the last 650 years, he still felt trapped. He would often come to the edge to look at what he could not have. He'd watch the little girl playing in her yard and long to be able to join her, in his boy or wolf form. It didn't matter, he just longed to be free. He had family but he longed for friendship and he felt a connection to that particular little girl. Not that he'd seen any other girls before, but there was something about this girl that made him happy when he watched her.

He'd come so close to getting her to enter the

forest that day when her mother came running and screaming at her to get away. He didn't know why she was going so crazy at the time, but now he did. He was just as anxious as Cassandra to learn more of the story and he was so glad he had not accomplished his goal that day. He never intended to trap her. All hope would have been lost had his selfishness prevailed. He wanted her to get started as well. He wanted to help her any way he could. He wondered if maybe he should look for Zythora's tomb. Surely he could find the center of Drenidore; but then what would he do? If he did something wrong, it could make matters worse than they were. But if he could do something to help, then freedom might be expedited. He'd have to think long and hard about how he could help and would definitely offer his services to her and her mother.

He was trying hard not to get excited at what he had learned and the prospect of destroying Zythora, because he knew it would be several years before Cassandra would be strong enough in her magic and have learned enough to make the attempt; plus the fact it had to be on her 16th birthday definitely guaranteed it would be a little over three years away.

He knew there was no magic in Drenidore because of the curse, but somehow he had managed to call to Cassandra, was it her magic that allowed it? His mind suddenly leaped to Zythora. It wasn't his call she had heard, it was Zythora's. Had she been able to get Cassandra to enter the woods, then her magic would have been lost due to the curse. She was afraid. Zythora was afraid! Oh my, Cassandra must be the one if Zythora was trying to prevent her becoming a full-fledged witch with all her powers intact. Maybe Cassandra could work through them and they would be able to help her in her quest. He needed to find Queen Angelica and tell her plans were underway to save them all from the curse. She might know of a way to help them. She may also know of a way to stop Zythora from creating any further havoc, or curses from her place of banishment. If she had enough power to call out, then she may have regained enough power to cause other problems as well.

Javan took off in a run. He was quite powerful in his wolf form and he would make good time as well as burn up some of the intenseness he was feeling and the overwhelming sense of urgency he felt when he thought of Zythora. He didn't really fear her at the moment, but he did believe she was definitely still a threat to them all. What if she could regain enough power to break free from the curse placed upon her by Lorissa?

He didn't have to run too long to reach the queen's palace. She was attending to flowers in her courtyard when he approached.

Javan, it is so good to see you, but why are you in such a rush?

It's Zythora, she's trying to stop the curse from being lifted from our kingdoms. I believe she's regaining her strength as she has called out to a young witch who has just discovered she has the potential to defeat and destroy Zythora once and for all. We need to do all we can to help her in her journey and I knew if anyone could be of assistance, it would be you. I know how much you loved your King and how happy you once were. I know how love was taken from you and our magic drained, along with joy and happiness. I know it's been a long six hundred and fifty years for you, but I also know and believe in my heart from what I have learned and felt this day that our savior has come in the form of a beautiful 12 year old girl named Cassandra. She is about to start training and she has the heart of a warrior. She feels so much for our people, animals and creatures she will stop at nothing to fulfill her destiny and save us all.

Javan, you may be right about this young witch being able to save us, but for Zythora to call out to her is unthinkable and very serious. The curse stripped her of her powers until Lorissa was dead or she herself was destroyed, thus breaking the curse.

She began pacing as she thought and Javan sat on her bench to watch and think as well. He didn't know what to think now. So he waited for his queen to formulate a question or theory about what was happening. He decided to work in her flower bed for her. He gently dug some weeds loose and pulled them out with his teeth, then patted the soil back around the flowers. He had done about a dozen plants with he heard her scream.

OH NO! Javan this is more serious than I thought. Lorissa must be ill. There is no other way for Zythora's strength to be restored. If Lorissa dies, her spell is voided due to the wording. Now witches usually have to be very old before they die, unless they are killed, so I'm sure she thought she would live long enough to find a way to kill Zythora, but she's either getting too old, or someone is speeding her death along. Quickly, we must get to the forest's edge and talk to Cassandra and her mother. They must find Lorissa and see to her well-being. If she dies, we're all doomed forever! Lead the way to her house. I'll be right behind you.

Javan ran as fast as he could towards

Cassandra's house. When they reached the edge of the forest, Javan started howling. He had howled for about ten minutes before Cassandra came outside to look into the forest.

Mama, that wolf is back at the edge of the forest, he's moving his head like he's motioning me to come there.

Wait Cassandra, let me see. What or who is that? Oh, there's a fairy with him.

They both walked down through the yard towards the forest. When they got close enough, Cassandra could see Javan in his boy form and Angelica motioned for them to come closer.

Miranda took Cassandra's hand and came within five feet of the edge, introduced herself, and asked what they wanted.

I am Angelica, Queen of Drenidore. This is Javan. He has come to me explaining that Cassandra will be our savior in less than four years, but he also said she was feeling a call. As we have no magic, and I mean no magic, I cannot even fly anymore; it has to be Zythora. Miranda, if she's gaining strength it can only mean one thing; Lorissa is ill and may be dying. You have to find her and keep her alive until Cassandra's 16th birthday when she can destroy Zythora. I don't know if some human or witch is the cause, but Lorissa is in danger and if she dies, we are all doomed. Please hurry and do all you can to save her. If there's anything we can do from in here, we will, but we're mainly powerless to help. I wish you God-speed and I thank you both for all you are going to do to save our worlds. We will always be indebted to you for this. Now go! Hurry! Time is fleeting! Save your Queen!

Miranda nodded, turned and pulled Cassandra along with her towards the house. After just a few steps, they were both running.

How will we know if they made it?

We'll still be alive this time next week. If they don't, the queen will die and Zythora will arise and wreak havoc on the entire world; starting with Drenidore and everyone and everything in it. She will arise with more vengeance than she had when she cursed us all. We will all know if they don't make it. If they do make it, we'll have a little over three years of hope that Cassandra and the white witches will be able to destroy her before she can gain enough power to rise again.

Can we do anything to help seal her tomb any tighter? Put something there so no one can mistakenly remove the chains or whatever is holding the spell in place? Anything would make me feel better. I hate being trapped and not being able to do anything. Waiting, waiting, and more waiting is not much fun!

Keep watch Javan and if you see them return home at any time, come get me and we'll talk to them to see if the lock on her tomb can be strengthened any. You are right to want to do that. We cannot let anyone mistakenly open her box. We have to educate everyone inside Drenidore on the dangers there and not leave anything for anyone to question so their curiosity won't get the better of them.

8 – Lorissa

Come Cassandra, we must hurry. They are correct, we have to get to Lorissa before she gets any worse. I know for a fact she's not that old, so someone is interfering with her life force and we can't have that.

They ran to the house, Miranda started throwing clothes and some food into a couple bags. Cassandra put on her walking shoes and grabbed their coats in case where they were going had bad weather. They both worked in silence. It took them less than a half hour to be ready to leave. Miranda gave everything a quick glance and decided they had what they needed. So they headed out the door and off on their journey.

Mama, how far do we have to go to get to Lorissa's house?

Castle, darling. She lives in a castle. She is the queen of the white witches, or good witches as some call us. She is our leader and we must follow any rules or decrees she makes. She is very powerful, but I fear Angelica may be right about her being in danger. Oh and to answer your question, it's about two days journey to the west. We will stop and gather witches along the way for support and power should we need it. I'm already sending out mental messages to those close to us. At the first cottage, I'll send out messages by carrier pigeon. We have to gather a coven, which is at least seven witches, in order to have enough power to undo whatever is happening to her.

Can we not just do magic and get there faster?

You mean like ride a broom? We don't do that type thing. Those are silly stories humans make up about us because they do not understand our powers and try to make light of them. If most humans knew what we can really do, they'd be scared witless. We can disappear and reappear somewhere else, but it's hard for us to take a passenger with us and you're not trained for that yet. It also cannot be an extremely long distance. We'll just have to go as fast as we can and hope someone down the line has some horses we can use to speed our journey. Right now we'll walk as fast as we can for as long as we can, then take a short rest, eat and move on. The closest witch is about eight hours away. They already know we're coming and have sent word to the next in line down the road and so on. Our forces are gathering as we speak. Once the last one receives a message back from Lorissa, then that will be passed all the way back to us. It takes a little while as there are several witches to pass through, but we will know by the time we reach our first stop. I'm sure she'll be trying to gather us some better transportation. The ones on down the line, will grab what they must have and start on their way to the castle. We'll be among the very last to arrive, but that's ok. Things will be in the works when we get there.

What if we don't get there in time?

If we don't make it in time, there will be no time. Zythora will take over the entire world and destroy anyone in her path that is not 100% backing her. Since we can't back her, we'll be destroyed. I think whatever or whoever it is that's poisoning her is purposefully taking it slowly. That way by the time she realizes what's happening to her Lorissa will be too weak to do much to stop them. If we can get there quick enough, we can help her recharge her magic and regain control of anything thrown off kilter. You're doing a great job keeping up sweetheart. I know it's going to be a hard journey for you.

Look mama, some horses in that field. Can we take them and then send them back when we're done?

Yes dear, we can but we'll need to bestow a gift upon the farmer who owns them. Do you know what we might give him?

We didn't bring much with us, so I'm really not

sure what we could do.

I think he might need a new roof on that barn over there. Can you concentrate on some boards and tin for me. Just think about them really hard and say these words. "Oh powers of the earth and sky, lend me your resources. I desire wood and tin to restore this barn. So mote it be done for me."

Carissa imagined the materials in her mind and said the words and voila! There appeared stacks of wood and tin.

Great that was your second spell! You're a fast learner. Now I'll do the rest. She spoke her spell and the wood and tin started flying to the top of the barn. Damaged rafters were replaced and covered in tin in a matter of seconds. "Now, let's get those horses.

They each extended their hands towards a horse and they accepted, became very willing and gentle. They climbed on and started at an easy gallop in the direction of the castle. Having the horses would cut their time in half and the horses would not even get tired. They actually reached the first witch in five hours instead of eight. She did have fresh horses waiting so they filled their canteens, switched horses, sent their horses back home to the farmer, and started off. Parisa handed them some jerky and apples to stave off their stomachs and they ate as they traveled. They each ate their snacks and enjoyed the means of travel while letting their feet and legs rest. It was only a short time before they came upon Seraphina, the next witch headed to the castle. She joined Cassandra on her horse and they returned the horses to a gallop so they were traveling at a good pace again.

Cassandra you met Parisa at our first stop, this is Seraphina. The next witch you'll meet will be Ariel and the others will be Evangeline, Laila and Melek. I told you we had to have at least seven in our coven present to help Lorissa. Oh and before you ask, yes they're all named after angels. I really don't think any children since the curse have been given any other names. Remember I told you how important that was.

I remember mama and I'm so excited to meet so many witches and to do more spells. I know they'll be easy ones, but I still can't wait!

They rode in silence till dark and they made camp. They fed the horses some apples and tied them to branches where they could eat some grass as well. Miranda brought out the sandwiches she'd made and some vegetables she had gathered from the garden that morning. It was a pretty good meal with some grape juice Parisa had brought that wasn't fermenting yet and cheese provided by Seraphina. As soon as they'd finished eating they stretched their mats out on the ground and lay down to sleep, they would be up at dawn to finish their journey and needed to be rested for it.

They were all tired and slept very well. Miranda was the first to wake and she used her magic to start a fire. She mixed some dough and fried some bread over the fire. She'd brought honey and jam so that was their breakfast. They ate quickly, rolled up their mats and were on their way. Time was of the essence so there was no lingering or unnecessary chit-chat. They had to be off as quickly as possible.

They were making great time with the horses and even ran them pretty hard when it was getting close to lunch time. They could rest while everyone ate a quick meal, then they would be off again, nearing the castle. They should make it there by midafternoon at the latest. They were already receiving messages from the other four witches. They had reached Lorissa and found her alone and very weak. Apparently she had been poisoned and left to die. They were pretty sure they could save her, but needed everyone to be there for the final spell.

She wasn't coherent enough for them to

discover who had poisoned her or what they had used. They were shooting questions back and forth trying to gather enough information to figure out the poison without actually being there. What color was she? Did she have a fever? Was there blood anywhere? What did her breath smell like? Were there any bite marks on her skin?

Miranda was repeating the messages she received so everyone could consider and help figure out what the poison was. She couldn't see. Her lips and tongue were burning and she had severe pain in her throat. Severe belly pain and her heartbeat was faint. Her skin was bluish and she smelled of violets.

It's turpentine poisoning Miranda shot back. She needs lots of fluids to flush it out, give her milk though instead of water. Drag her bed or wherever she is close to the door or window to give her fresh air. We're close. I'm sending the other witches ahead and I'll be there with Cassandra as quickly as I can. Sisters, use your magic to transport to the castle and begin casting some spells to restore her strength and ease her pain. We'll be there as quickly as possible.

They all disappeared, leaving Miranda and Cassandra alone with all the horses. Miranda uttered a spell for the empty horses to follow them and then she put a spell on their horses to strengthen their legs and give them added speed.   Hold on Cassandra, they're going to go faster. Our time is short. We have to get Lorissa over this poisoning and fast!

You'd have thought those were race horses they were riding and they were just a half hour behind the others when they arrived.

We had to force her to drink the milk, but it has helped her be able to speak. We've stopped the pain in her belly and she's breathing better when we got her fresh air. I cast a spell on the curtains to flap and flap, drawing in the fresh air and moving it directly towards her face.

You've done a great job Parisa, now let's all join hands and finish this task. I'll do the spell while the rest of you chant. Cassandra, you join in too; just say the words and see your power in your mind moving from you into the circle. Cassandra nodded and grabbed hands and began chanting the same as she'd been told they had done when all their problems started so many years ago.

Powers that be, give us the power
Powers of light, expel the darkness
Powers that be, give us the power
Powers of light, expel the darkness.

Miranda uttered the spell to heal Lorissa and give her strength.

"I call upon the Gods and Goddesses to give me strength and power to overcome this wicked evil which has afflicted our queen. Give us the power to defeat it. I command that this poison be removed from her body, strength from the coven be transferred to her and her body join in the fight to rid her of this poison and treachery done her. Reveal unto us who committed this crime against our queen and I command this poison to enter into the body who gave it her and afflict them sorely. Do this for me. So Mote It Be."

Miranda spoke the spell three times before Lorissa opened her eyes and stopped crying in pain. They all became silent and Miranda looked around the circle and back at Lorissa before speaking. "Lorissa, did you have a fight with your daughter? I know she is the one who did this as it was revealed during the spell."

I did. She wanted my kingdom and I told her she wasn't ready. She said she'd made a deal with someone that would give her rule over much if she eliminated the current queen. I don't know how or when she had communicated with Zythora, but apparently she had. I love my daughter and cannot believe she betrayed me of her own free will, but I also know she is strong willed and has wanted my kingdom for a great many years. I find sorrow in knowing she did this to me and more sorrow in knowing that the spell was cast that she receive the poison from my body and it is now happening to her. I know the pain she'll endure and she's all alone, but I feel proper judgement has been executed and I hold no ill will towards any of you. Thank you, my great and loyal subjects, for saving me. Now let me rest and grieve for my lost daughter, for I still love her no matter what evil she did to me.

You are most welcome our beloved queen, but I want you to know that Queen Angelica and one of her changelings, I'm sorry I never asked his name, brought it to our attention.

Mama, she said his name was Javan.

That's right she did. Well without them, we'd have never reached you in time. You see Zythora was calling out to my daughter Cassandra trying to get her to enter the woods. She is the chosen one and Zythora somehow knows it. She was regaining strength as you were dying. We've stopped that, but if you grant us permission, we will remain here and train Cassandra until her 16th birthday that she may speak the spell to break the curse. Our remaining together will help ensure that our coven will be strong and we'll give her our strength to do it. We will then be free from Zythora forever!

Of course you may stay my sweet Miranda. Had you not sounded the alarm and raised the troops, if you will, I would be dead by now. I owe you a debt and will not forget it any time soon.

I appreciate having protectors here for me and company as this witch has been alone for way to long. I will especially enjoy having a witch in training in my household. Now I'm going to rest as I can barely hold my head up any longer and I'll see you in the morning. I think I'll rest through supper; but please, all of you, make yourselves at home. Eat, take rest, enjoy anything you desire. My home is your home now.

Cassandra walked over to where Lorissa lay and she reached out and took her hand, smiled, and kissed her knuckles. I am here, your highness, and I will do whatever I can to protect you from any harm our enemies might think to bring against you.

Thank you my child. I look forward to spending time with you after I've rested and mourned my daughter. You've raised her well Miranda.

Thank you my queen, she is a prize for certain.

9 – Training

Cassandra, you need to have a fundamental understanding of what magic really is before you can effectively use it. Here's a pad, make yourself some notes as we go. You'll need to refer to them often.

Magic is more than speaking a spell. It is raising and channeling energy. The energy is found in many places. From within yourself, at random in nature, in fellow witches and in the divine deities. You can use any or all of these energies to achieve your desires. You just need to know how to access them and channel them for your individual purpose.

In gaining access to another's powers, you will need to ask. Like the chanting by others in the coven. You have asked them to chant for you and thus when that begins their power is channeled through you along with any powers they receive from the deities they're chanting to. If you want powers from the deities, you invoke them asking for their powers. Like I said in the spell for Lorissa I said "I call upon the Gods and Goddesses to give me strength and power" it's that simple to receive their help. Power from nature comes from asking the wind, the water, the air, the trees, the plants and even the animals for their power and assistance, much like you ask the gods for it.

Once you have the power channeled to you, then you direct that power where you want it to go by finishing the spell you're casting and telling that energy or power where to go and what to do. You command it by giving direction to it and telling it to do it for you. Confirming the spell is when I said "So Mote It Be." Or please allow this to happen, I must have it. Is sort of what that phrase means.

It is your ethical duty to use your power responsively. You are responsible for your actions and every spell you cast. If you injure someone willingly the penalty you'll pay is steeper than if it's an accident; however you are also responsible for accidents too, so choose wisely when, where, and what to use magic for.

You need to learn how the phases of the moon affect your powers. Always keep track of the waxing and waning of the moon. You never know when you'll need to use a spell and when you'll need help executing it due to lack of power and how it affects your mood and body. During a waxing moon, or when it's getting full, your power will build to its strongest as the moon builds. When it's full, you will be your strongest. When the moon is losing size and going into the no moon phase, your power will decrease. Don't try to defeat a strong witch on your weakest day, you'll need help to accomplish that goal. Try a simple spell when you are most powerful and try the same spell when you are your weakest. You may have to repeat the spell, unless it's extremely simple.

You are born a witch, but you also must choose it. You have felt the call and have chosen to be a witch. You also must choose whether to use your craft for good or evil. You have already chosen this as well. You chose to be a white witch and use your powers for good. Good for yourself, other witches and mankind as a whole. You are dedicating yourself to honing your skills and using the craft and this is the path you wish to pursue.

Remember I told you patience was important. Especially in training, you will have to use your patience. Persistence is also valuable as your powers are small and will need strengthening. They will grow the more you practice and learn your craft. You may have to try the same spell a dozen times before you get everything worked out, lined up and tuned in; but when you do, your spell will work.

Focus is another thing you must work on daily. When you can cast a spell in the middle of a hurricane, with a child in your arms and a scared animal tied to you, then you are focusing. You have to clearly see your objective and tune everything else out in order to make a spell work.

The skills you learn to do witchcraft are skills you can use every day of your life. Your schoolwork will improve, your friendships will improve, your life as a whole will improve. If you are focused on what you're trying to do, nothing can enter your space. Of course the real skill comes when you are that focused, but can still know what's going on around you. You certainly don't want to direct a lightning bolt at the door of our house to destroy a fly as that will cause destruction to something you need. You have to know where that fly landed. You also don't want to attack Zythora, for instance, if there's an innocent child behind her. You can't plow through her and not hurt the child. You have to be aware of everything around you but not let it distract you from accomplishing your goal.

I found when in training, that for me small exercises in concentrating and visualizing worked best. Like you did with the wood and tin, you visualized in your mind then spoke the words. When we finish with your outline today, I want you to spend twenty minutes visualizing things and making them appear. For instance four eggs for breakfast tomorrow. A block of chocolate for our dessert tonight. A lovely hat to keep the sun from your eyes and skin. A couple oranges for our afternoon snack. Get a bowl from the kitchen, take it outside and visualize a bowl of hot water, work on getting the temperature of that water where you would like it to be. Try cold, then warm like you were going to wash clothes. Then make some hot water for a bath and hot water for tea. They are both hot, so your mind has to change the temperature with more intense concentration. You don't want to use magic to draw your bath for tonight and use the temperature you would use for tea. It would burn your skin. And vice versa you wouldn't want anything less than boiling to brew your tea. It all takes practice. You'll do these things over and over until you perfect your concentration skills. The more focused you are the stronger your magic will be.

You need to learn to remain calm no matter what. You can be very still and hear the voice of the gods and goddesses when they call to you, or when they answer your call. If your mind is not calm or still, you'll miss it. If you are not focused, you won't hear or be heard. It's a balance you must work on because maintaining control is essential to utilizing your powers to their fullest.

When you cast a spell, it is much better for you to write your own. It will have your exact meaning built in so there's no mistaking your intentions. It will be harder for someone else to break or reverse and you will remember it. If you try to remember every spell you hear cast, you will fail. If you try to remember a spell you wrote and cast, you'll come much closer to remembering every syllable of it. However, casting someone else's spell will work for you too. Many witches write their spells in books and share them all the time. I know one witch who keeps two books, one to share with a friend when they get together, and that's fine but they are better used as guidelines for you to create your own rituals.

I am in a coven or circle as some call it because I need to work with them many times. I want to learn from them and I want to share things I've learned about a particular spell or need for a spell. Sometimes I leave out an important step and it just doesn't work. That's when an extra set of eyes on the subject can find what's wrong and help me with my spells. Here's an example of a spell reversal you can try this with me or one of the ladies. Choose something simple like having them give you a wart or a pimple. There are simple spells to remove those no matter who put them on you. But to test if you can reverse a spell, you have to have one put on you and giving someone a wart is a harmless spell.

Once you have the wart you can do a reversal as you know who put the hex on you. Here's the reversal spell:

Spell Reversal: Spell Bottle

To send a hex back when you know exactly where it came from.

1. Obtain personal items from your persecutor: hair, nail clippings, photo, letter, etc.

2. Put them inside a jar or a bottle with a cork.

3. Cut a piece of red cloth into a heart shape.

4. Stick pins into it. Visualize all the negative energy and enmity leaving you, like arrows, going back where they came from.

5. Stuff it into the bottle.

6. Add nails, pins, or needles.

7. Bury it in the ground.

And lastly' the time you spend every day should increase by five minutes. Today you will practice twenty minutes, tomorrow twenty-five, until you are up to eight hours in a day. You will use your magic to make your bed, wash your clothes, dry your clothes, fold your clothes and put them away. You will use magic to clean your room, do the dishes, sweep the kitchen, mop the kitchen, and dust the rugs. Every chore around the house, except for fire, will get a taste of your magic. Anything regarding fire will be done under strict supervision by me or one of the others in the coven. It is too easy for fire to get away from you while in training.

I have a questions mama. If I can produce something from nothing, why didn't you do that when we needed horses to get to Lorissa?

You needed training and had I spoken a spell you may have tried it on your own. You needed guidance and instruction before you started using your magic. I was protecting you from yourself and I was protecting anyone who might be anywhere near us.

OK mama, I understand, I think. I'm ready now to produce some eggs for breakfast.

I'm not going to stay and watch you so you can concentrate better and won't be nervous, but if you get into trouble, please shout and don't try to fix it yourself as you may create more problems than you already have. I have chores of my own to attend to, and I want to check on Lorissa too. I won't be far, just take your time and concentrate.

Miranda went about her chores and Cassandra took a deep breath, pictured eggs in her mind and spoke these words. **Sprits of the earth send to me eggs from a chicken for me to eat for breakfast tomorrow. So mote it be done for me.** When she opened her eyes there were two chickens on the table. I don't get it, she complained out loud. I thought of eggs. Oh, then I thought about tomorrow too much, these chickens will each lay me an egg by tomorrow.

I didn't ask for eggs for mama too or I might have had four chickens. She said to herself.

She put the chickens on the ground and thought about the eggs again, concentrated on eggs for her breakfast and spoke the words again. **Sprits of the earth send to me eggs from a chicken for me to eat. So mote it be done for me.** Oh my gosh! She exclaimed. Why was the wood and tin so easy, but getting eggs right is beyond me? She had two eggs for "her" to eat but they were cooked and ready to eat. Be specific mama said. Again she closed her eyes and thought about four eggs laying on the table in front of her. **Sprits of the earth send to me four chicken eggs to be cooked for my breakfast. So mote it be done for me.** She sort of peeked between her eyelids and saw four eggs laying in front of her just as she'd seen in her mind. YAY! I did it! She shouted. Maybe I'll do better with the chocolate.

Eyes closed, mind seriously thinking about chocolate, imagining the taste of it, smelling the aroma **Sprits of the earth send to me chocolate candy, oh so sweet. So mote it be done for me.** Alright! First try and she had imagined two big pieces and that's what was on the table. That one was easy; but she had thought much more about the chocolate, the color, the taste, the aroma. All these things added to her desires.

Oranges for our snack she said. Eyes closed, see the oranges, two of them. Smell the aroma, see the juice dripping down when I bite into it. **Sprits of the earth send to me two oranges ripe, juicy and sweet. So mote it be done for me.** Great! Another one first time. She continued with those things until she had enough eggs for breakfast all week, some deviled eggs for lunch and enough to bake a cake, and make pudding. She had enough oranges for their snack, orange juice for breakfast tomorrow and flavoring for that cake. She had enough chocolate for dessert, icing for the orange cake, and enough to melt and make some chocolate milk. She hadn't even started on the hat and water experiments yet, but she was very comfortable with the other items.

She decided if she was going to boil water, she may as well make tea, so she gathered cups and a pitcher for brewing tea and a couple bowls for trying different temperatures. These experiments went much faster towards success than the first ones had. She was more confident and didn't need to concentrate nearly as long to get it right and she got them right the first time every time and she even used a spell to get some sugar so she didn't have to go back in the house to drink her tea.

Miranda came to check on her after about an

hour and she very excitedly began telling her about her trials and successes. She even had a cup of tea with her and she took the pitcher of tea in to share with the coven. They all appreciated it and said it was the best tasting they'd ever had. Cassandra told them it was because it was brewed with magic. They laughed because they'd all used magic before to make tea or any food they needed or wanted appear but they let her believe it was her magic that made it so good.

Oh, and I have hats for all you ladies, different colors too. And PLEASE can I make lunch for everyone. I'm on a roll and would love to do it. I won't build a fire, I'll just make everything already cooked. Can I please? They consented and she had a spread fit for a king's table. She had four meats and not small portions. She'd cooked a whole ham, a whole leg of lamb, an entire side of beef and a very large turkey, twenty different side dishes, sauces, gravies and a whole table full of desserts. Every kind imaginable was there and some they hadn't imagined before.

Lorissa had them ring the bell and open the gates to let the villagers in so they could enjoy the meal. She would do something like that periodically to keep them happy and help supplement their food supply. She always made sure they had good crops, plenty of sunshine and rain, but not too harsh of weather to destroy anything. She insisted they had to work for their food. She didn't want them getting lazy and depending on someone else to take care of them. She told them she had a cook in training and she'd cooked everything in the pantry, so enjoy and eat all they wanted and take the leftovers home for tomorrow. It was a grand feast and Cassandra enjoyed meeting the people and talking with them. She and her mother had been alone for so long, she barely knew how to approach someone to make friends.

It was a great first day of being a witch. They were all so proud of her and the villagers were happy too, knowing all was well in their world and the power of the witches was still being used for the good of everyone. Some of them actually believed that the witches thought they didn't know about their powers. It was a little game they all played, pretending everything and everyone was a normal human being instead of a few witches thrown in. The town folk didn't mind as they benefitted from their powers and they didn't want to lose that.

Training would continue tomorrow. With more surprises, she was sure.

10 – Training Continues

It was more exciting every day for Cassandra. She was truly a fast learner and she had confidence in herself and a strong will to succeed. She wanted to be the best witch ever and grow strong enough to destroy Zythora herself, but she'd never be cocky enough to believe that she didn't need help from her coven. This was too important to take any unnecessary chances. She read spell books and began writing her own spells and practicing them on a daily basis. She began with small things and would work up as her powers grew and as she had the desire to test them on other people and witches.

She found it very fun to make things appear. She had taken to providing all the meals by magic with some very elaborate desserts with fancy details. One day she made a cake that was an exact replica of the castle. It contained twelve different flavors inside and was fifteen feet long, nine feet wide and eleven feet tall. Once the other witches had seen it, they decided it must go to the village. So Cassandra loaded it on a wagon pulled by four beautiful white Arabian horses and they all went into town to share the bounty with the locals.

They pulled their wagon into the town square and began ringing the bell that was used for special announcements and such. They had brought five hundred large chargers so everyone could take home the equivalent of a whole cake after they had all eaten their fill there in the square. Cassandra produced punch and ale for everyone including goblets. They had two additional wagons besides the one with the cake.

The children were going crazy over just the sight of it all; and everyone enjoyed the party. The ladies were thankful to have such an elaborate treat for the remainder of the week and the men were all enjoying the ale; maybe a little too much. It didn't matter, though, they were all happy.

They knew it was witches who ruled this village, but they also knew their lives were better for it. They were given many things and protection by the witches as well. It wasn't an easy life, they still had to work for what they had, but they didn't have to worry that their crops would fail or about natural disasters taking their homes. They planted, hoed and harvested every season and they were rewarded for their efforts. They were happy and enjoyed the pleasures it afforded them.

They had no knowledge of how fragile their lives really were and if their plan of destroying Zythora failed how miserable their existences would become. But that was something the witches would work on, never letting them know there was any real danger. They did love the villagers and were never threatened or annoyed by their fears or suspicions like so many other kingdoms had to endure. They didn't have to erase their memory or hide their presence or castle even, they were embraced by the people so they embraced them right back.

Cassandra wanted to do something every day or week for the people but Lorissa told her that she couldn't. They couldn't risk the people becoming dependent upon their generosity. They would get lazy and if anything ever happened to the witches, then they wouldn't be able to survive. This saddened Cassandra, but she did tell her that she could go to school with the other children, if it didn't interfere with her studies at home. She could not use magic at school, but would take her lunch and do her homework just like every other child there. They all agreed it would provide her some much needed company and social skills that she was lacking when having to deal with someone her own age, or having the empathy to relate on a different level. This made her so happy and she was ready bright and early the next morning. She ran in to kiss her mother good-bye and was so disappointed when Miranda smiled and told her there was no school today as it was Saturday. She'd have to wait till Monday to begin school, but maybe she could go into town to play in the park and maybe meet some children and make a friend or two.

We'll take a picnic lunch and go for a while. We'll take a couple extra sandwiches just in case if you want. What would you like to take with you to play? A jump rope maybe or a ball to kick around?

Can I take both mama? So whatever someone wants to play, I'll be ready.

Of course, now let's see some magic skills from you while we wait until time to prepare our lunch and enjoy the beautiful day that it seems we're going to have.

So Cassandra made some more things appear...rabbits, goats, a couple more horses, a barn full of hay and corn to feed them all. She was excited to have pets as she'd never had any before. It was all so new and exhilarating. She could pretty much do whatever she wanted. She produced new clothes, fancy curtains and linens for her bed. Miranda cautioned her that she was appearing to be spoiled and verging on being a brat and those were things that no one really appreciated.

She moved on to fixing some things that needed repairing instead of making new things appear. She was becoming quite the carpenter. Miranda made sure she understood that she needed knowledge of how things worked in order to fix them. Many times it was better to mend than make; as a witch couldn't always be so free and needed to remain less conspicuous to the world around them. Cassandra liked fixing things. It was more of a challenge for her. She'd repaired any bumps and dings in the walls and then painted the entire castle inside and out. She'd repaired any squeaking or broken boards. Sanded and stained all the woodwork and changed much of the artwork. Everything else got a thorough cleaning. She used a cloth and her powers, but she watched the cloth go over every surface. She liked decorating too. Everything was so bright and cheery in the entire castle so she decided to continue working outside.

She tackled the gardens. All the hedges were trimmed, dead plants uprooted and replanted, trees were trimmed and flower beds cleaned out, soil was fertilized and they were replanted or whatever else they needed.

Mother, is there anything you know of that needs done. I can't find anything else to work on.

You have done a magnificent job cleaning, repairing, and sprucing up the entire castle as well as doing the laundry, cooking and general housekeeping, but what you haven't done is exercise your mind and body.

What? My mind is all that's really worked.

Not really, dear. Your magic has worked, but your mind has little to do with looking at something and imagining what you want done to it and doing it. You have other skills you need to develop. You live in a world that is not just for witches or just about witches. You will not always be around people who accept you for what you are. There are many places where they want to destroy you for what you are, not who you are. You need to work your mind to figure people out and your body in fitting in. I want you to start working in town to fix things up without using your magic. I want you to find someone to tutor you in some sort of craft or skill that you can accomplish with your hands to benefit someone else.

How will I do that?

You talk to people after school. You might start with your teacher. She may need the erasers dusted or a chair repaired. She might like her room cleaned and painted (with your hands to see just what's involved in doing it rather than speaking it done). The janitor may need help and you could mop the floors for real, not just with magic. That is something you use your hands for. Yes it won't be as spotless and will take much longer, but you will learn the value of working. It truly is valuable for you to learn how the rest of the world lives without magic. Then you can understand those who dislike you because they are jealous of you for your magic; or those who are mad because they cannot do the things you do and they think they've been cheated out of something that should have been theirs. Really, why you and not them? If you're going to understand people, you need to live like them, at least for a while, so you'll know what it's like to have worked all day and then come home and have to work some more. Maybe going to bed hungry because the food was burned because you had to tend to a sick child and couldn't pay close enough attention to the fire. All those things happen to humans and much more. It's hard to wash the dishes when you have blisters on your hands from hoeing the corn or pulling weeds all day from the garden or flower beds, and didn't have any gloves to wear.

Oh, I know a good project. The town square needs spruced up, the hedges trimmed, new flowers planted, the clock and bell probably need painted too. Ask around to see who you can get to help you. Offer to help them do something in exchange for their time to help you do your project. You might even work for someone in town to earn money to buy the flowers and paint. People will see what you're doing and appreciate you for it. They won't just see a hand out from your magic, like the cake; but they'll see you giving a hand where it's needed. Actually going out of your way and exerting some sweat and muscles to get the job done.

This type training doesn't seem nearly as fun as the first things I was doing, but if you think it's important, I'll work on it.

It is important. Now, let's get our lunch packed so we can go play in the park for a while and maybe meet some children while we're there.

They packed their lunch and toys in a bag and headed off for the village. They found several children already at play when they arrived. They were about her age and were dressed very plainly. Their clothes were not tattered but they were very worn and you could tell they'd been patched and repaired. Cassandra smiled at her mother, took the ball and jump rope, then headed towards a small group of girls as her mother sat on a bench in the shade to watch.

Do you girls want to play ball with me?

Sure! They all exclaimed and began making comments on how pretty the ball was. One girl said the only ball they'd ever gotten to play with was hard. They could throw it to play catch, but it didn't bounce like this one did. They played for a while and then the girls showed her how to sing rhyming songs while they clapped hands with each other. She had good rhythm so it didn't take her long to be able to keep up. There were different rhythms and different songs, so they did that for a while and then they played on the teeter totter and swings.

Miranda watched her little girl truly be a little girl full of life and happiness with other children her age. There were four of them and only two extra sandwiches so she did a little magic of her own and produced two more sandwiches and a bowl of pudding and six spoons for dessert. Cassandra would be excited as well since she'd packed apples. But she knew they would all love the pudding and could have the apples as well before they finished playing.

It was almost lunchtime and she wanted to make sure none of them took off for home before they could share with them, so she called to them to come over for lunch. She spread a large table cloth on the ground as they were coming and laid the plate of sandwiches out with the bag of apples and the bowl of pudding. All the girls came running over and their eyes lit up when they saw the food, especially the pudding. She told them to help themselves to a sandwich while she dished up the pudding. They were adorable all sitting along the edges of her table cloth. Cassandra never looked happier. They had almost finished eating when two of their mothers came across to where they were all sitting.

Girls, you knew we would be coming to get you for lunch and yet you've eaten already. They squealed that Cassandra had brought extra to share and they had pudding! The women smiled at Miranda and she gestured for them to sit down and dismissed the girls to play some more. She produced a bag of marbles to keep them amused and even Cassandra's eyes were full of excitement at the sight of them.

Ladies, I'm sorry if I interrupted your lunch plans, but I do have apples left if you'd like a snack. We have not been here too long and my daughter is lonely for playmates. She starts school on Monday so we thought we might introduce ourselves and make a friend or two so the first day wouldn't be too hard.

That is so thoughtful of you. My name is Mary and my friend here is Tabitha. We'll encourage our girls to remember when it was their first day and how scared they were. She won't have any problem adjusting to a new school or making friends, especially if she keeps bringing pudding. We never seem to have enough eggs and milk to make pudding.

Oh, I can help with that, we really have too many chickens and I can even give you a cow. Cassandra seems to attract animals and our chickens hatched two dozen chicks each last year so we're up to fifty chickens. That's why we made the pudding—too many eggs. Which house is yours and we'll bring some into town as we come to school Monday. Oh, and is it appropriate here for the children to assist in feeding the teacher or do we pay or both? I hadn't had time to check, but didn't want to show up empty handed if I needed to bring something.

I think she might love a couple chickens, we all usually share what we have and our husbands keep her house fixed up as well as the school house. There are only a couple families in town that can pay. She's a lovely young woman and seems to get by on whatever it is that is given her. I've never seen her with an abundance of anything, but she's never been hungry either. She's a beautiful seamstress. She can hem a dress and you'll never see a stitch. It's amazing really. That should have been her calling, she might have made money doing it, but she loves the children and treats every single one of them like they're her own.

I appreciate your advice Tabitha. I make soap and perfumes from the flowers we grow in the gardens. I'll bring her some of that, the chickens and a couple coins as well, since I sell the perfumes and manage to earn enough to take care of my daughter and myself rather well. Maybe it will be a good thing we're here to help out a little where times are tough.

She may argue it's too much, but really if you can be so generous I know she'll appreciate the luxuries. She's a kind soul, don't you agree Mary?

Definitely. We are blessed to have her teaching our children. We're also happy to have had the chance to chat with you and get to know you and Cassandra a bit more. I think our girls are going to be forever friends. They all smiled and watched the girls playing like they'd known each other for years. Finally the ladies decided they'd better get home, housework and dinner was calling them. They thanked her for their children's lunch as well as the apples they'd eaten.

Please take the rest home with you. Maybe you can make a pie or some tarts with them for your supper. Our trees are loaded this year. Does either of you by any chance make juice or cider? I'd love to have some help making some. I've never done it by myself. My mother used to do it and I'd help. I'd be happy to share on the halves with you. Just bring jars or jugs to put yours in. I have some extra containers too, if you don't have enough. We'll make some for the teacher as well. Any takers?

They both laughed and said they'd love to do that and Monday would be good for them if that was ok with me.

I assured them it would and we agreed it was a date then. They turned to leave and I stopped them. If you think six or seven more ladies would like the same offer, we could make apple butter as well and maybe bake some pies while we are at it for our dinners. If that many of us work together it will take us most of the day, but we'll have a large assortment for everyone to take home, plus some fresh apples too.

We'll bring some more of the ladies. I'm sure they'll love meeting you too. They waved goodbye as I called for Cassandra to gather her things, say goodbye and we would be heading home.

I may have made some friends today as well dear. I've invited nine ladies to make apple butter, cider, juice and pies on Monday while you girls are in school.

This is a good place to live mama. I like those girls and they seem to like me. I can't wait for school on Monday.

Just remember dear, all the children won't like you. Some will be afraid, some will be jealous and some just won't like you because they don't like anyone or anything that's new or different. Remind me to send soap and a couple coins for your teacher on Monday. We'll take her a couple chickens, some more soap and some perfume when we both can go visit her. We'll try to do that Tuesday since I'll be busy all day Monday. Plus, I'll have apple butter, juice, cider, and a pie to take her then too. Everyone seems to love her and if we can make her life a little more enjoyable, we'll be happy doing it. I hope you always love helping people as much as I do. It makes me so happy to bring joy to someone else.

11 – School and friends

Cassandra, it's time to get up for school. Miranda set a plate of pancakes on the table with some fruit juice, molasses, and butter, she'd used magic that morning but would not for most of the day. She was used to doing things like the humans. She had raised Cassandra without magic in her life so a hard day's work was very commonplace for Miranda. While Cassandra got ready for school Miranda got ready for their guests to come. She pulled out the long tables, knives, bowls, the two copper kettles for making apple butter, jars, jugs, and the tubs they would need to boil water in for cleaning jars, washing the fruit and making the mash in. She waved to her daughter leaving and the nine ladies arriving. They were all pushing wheel barrows filled to the brim. Everyone looked in a jolly mood to start their day off.

As the ladies unloaded their respective jars, jugs, knives and baskets, Miranda was still busy getting everything out. They immediately introduced themselves and split up into groups. The apple butter had to be started first, as it would take all day to cook, put in jars and let seal; so, they figured if they all gathered a basket of apples, peeled that basketful, cut it and got it in the kettles, then moved on to the other items while a couple kept watch on those pots and began adding the spices to get the apple butter going, they would be able to accomplish all they wanted.

All the ladies loaded into the wagon with their baskets and Miranda drove them to the orchard. There were forty-five trees in the orchard and each one was loaded with ripe apples. Everyone worked like they'd been a team for years. When all their baskets were full, they hopped back in the wagon and headed back to the outdoor kitchen to start pealing. Fires were built and apples were cooking when half the group headed back to the orchard, the rest tended the kettles, washed all the containers they would be using and had everything ready for the next steps.

When the ladies came back with all the baskets full of apples again, half of those stayed to start peeling, and cutting apples to go into the press. The peelings, and pulp from the press, were thrown into a big tub with some water and were started cooking too; this would be what they made the cider from. They made juice from the apples and cider from the pulp, peelings and scraps as it would be strained and then it had to ferment for a couple of days before it would be ready to drink. The other half went back to the orchard to gather more apples.

This time when they returned, they sorted the apples. The best ones with no blemishes were placed in sacks of fifty for each woman to take home for the family to eat. The rest they started peeling to make pies. Each woman had brought three tins to put pies in. Miranda took two of the ladies into the cellar with her. They loaded a wheelbarrow with bags of flour and sugar and took to the outside kitchen. She gathered the spices and the lard for the pies, bowls, table clothes to work on and rolling pins and then went to work with the ladies baking pies. They laughed and joked all day, but they worked non-stop except to eat lunch and then someone still had to be stirring the apple butter.

It was a hard day, but these women were used to hard days. It was much easier when you had someone to work with and you were getting all your ingredients for free. They each told her a little about themselves and their families throughout the day and they all laughed, smiled, and even sang a bit as they worked.

It was about three when the children came walking up the hill. They were just as happy as the women were. There were seven girls and eight boys in the group. They all ran to their respective mothers and gave them a hug then they all wanted to know if there was something they could eat.

Come in the house children, I have bread, cheese, and meat for your snack. It was good when we ate it at lunch so you should enjoy it as well. There is also cake that Cassandra made last night and we have grape juice, apple juice, and milk, so whatever your choice is, feel free to eat and drink all you want.

It was another two hours before everything was finished and the wagon was being loaded. The children had jumped in and helped do what they could too. The cleaning up, wiping jars, carrying stuff to the respective wheel barrows or the wagon. It didn't matter they were happy and used to working hard too to help their families. The big wagon that had carried the cake before, was filled to the brim. The ladies loaded their portions in the wagon according to the order of who's stop was last to first, so they wouldn't have to climb over anyone to get their stuff. The things for the school teacher were placed in line with everyone else's. Each child carried a chicken to take home with them and Cassandra carried two for their teacher. I love Ms. Catherine mama, she is so pretty and so nice too. I'm glad we're taking some stuff to her. Did you remember the soap and perfume?

Yes, I did, sweetheart, and I sneaked a bar of soap in each of the ladies' bags where they placed their aprons. I've had a wonderful day and I am so glad we are living here now.

Once they'd delivered everyone and all their stuff home, including Ms. Catherine's, (Who, by the way, thanked all the ladies for their part in making all her wonderful goodies and especially Miranda and Cassandra. Miranda told her to send word when she could come for dinner and they'd get better acquainted too.) they returned home to put their things away.

Now, when you're looking for odd jobs to do this week, you keep a look out for any older folk who might live alone and we'll take them some of our apple goodies too. That might be another avenue for you to explore in finding a craft or skill to learn. Older people know a lot of stuff and if you will just spend time with them, you'll learn a lot. They love to talk and share their knowledge with anyone who will listen. That's another good piece of advice for you to remember and keep tucked away for later years. And always be respectful. I've taught you that and I don't want you to forget it. People will always like you if you're kind, honest and respectful.

Now that we've finished putting everything away, let's eat some pie for dinner and you can tell me about your first day at school.

Really? Pie for dinner?! This day just got even better! She was so excited, but she managed to tell everything that happened in school that day and was excited to go back. I'm just like all the other girls, mama; no one knows I'm a witch, I fit right in, and everyone likes me, even the boys! Well except for Millie Jenkins. She is the Town Maester's daughter and she thinks she's the best thing since butter. No one likes her very much, she's a know-it-all and makes fun of people's clothes, and stuff. She shouldn't act like they're no good because they're poor. I bet her daddy doesn't have nearly as much money as she lets on.

It doesn't matter dear; you treat her just like everyone else. You be kind and honest and respectful, just like I've taught you.

It sure is hard mama when she says nasty things about other kids. I really would like to smack her and tell her she's not so special. I know lots of people richer than she is.

Now...

I know! I'll be as nice as I can, but let me tell you when I earn some money someday, I'm going to buy some nicer clothes for some of those kids so she won't be so mean to them.

She is probably the most miserable child in

town.

WHAT!?

I mean it. She probably thinks she has to act some certain way because her daddy is the Town Maester and because they don't really have any more than anyone else in town, it's hard for her to have the things she needs to look and act rich. You never know what someone else is going through. What if her fancy dresses are all she has, so she has to be careful and not enjoy playtime like the rest of you because she can't mess up her clothes. I bet her play clothes are torn and ragged and her night clothes are probably thread bare. She may not have the fancy life at all like she pretends. You should be extra nice to her.

Are you kidding me?

No, I mean it. I want you to be extra nice, if she'll let you. Offer her an apple or your pudding. Tell her you'd like to be her friend. She'll probably make fun of you, but you be ready for it. You'll know it has nothing to do with you, it's her problem she's dealing with. She may be the poorest girl in school and would be most ashamed if anyone found out. She'd not be able to live with it, so she has no friends who might invite her over to play or to sleep over. That way they'd never know how things were outside of what people see at school and in the open in town.

I'll try, but if she gets too mean I'll... Cassandra!

Yes, mama, I'll be nice.

Now let's get ready for bed, I'm tired. You can snuggle in with me if you want and tell me more about your day and your teacher and what you learned until one of us falls asleep.

She again stated how much she loved her teacher and everyone in school except Millie. They were studying arithmetic, division to be exact and they were reading some story about a king and queen who lived a long time ago. I think it must be made up because they have no servants or anyone else around them. They just had lots of rules and everyone had to obey those rules or get their heads chopped off.

Lunchtime was great, we got to play chase and ball. I liked them both. I also traded lunch with a little boy named Peter, I think he's really poor mama. He pulled his lunch out of his napkin and all he had was an egg. Just one. So, I looked at him and said. "Oh my goodness! You get to have an egg for lunch! I'm so jealous. I love eggs! You wouldn't want to trade, would you?" He was so unsure what to do, he said well what do you have to trade? I opened my napkin and said, "I have bread and cheese" and before I could say anything else he said ok so I just kept going; "and a piece of apple pie and a cup of juice. I hope that's ok." His eyes lit up and he handed me his egg and said that's more than enough, why don't we share the juice and pie. I know he was hungry mama, so I gave him the biggest piece of my pie and most of my juice. You are right, it's really hard for some of them. Maybe we can find a way to help him and his family.

I think we can. I'll ask your teacher when we have dinner this week and see what we can do.

I'm so proud of you honey for helping him and for making it seem like he was helping you. Sounds like it was his first good meal in a long time maybe. See if he will be your friend. We'll pack an extra something in your napkin for him to have with his egg. He wasn't a child of one of the women who came to work the apples, so his mother may be shunned by them as well, or she has a job somewhere and couldn't come. I think he may need a friend as much as Millie does.

Oh, her again, please don't tell me I have to ask her to be my friend. If I do I probably won't have any others because she won't be my friend and no one else will want to be because I asked her.

It will be ok, you'll see. Why don't you invite her to come on Saturday for tea. Tell her tea is usually fancy so she's probably the only kid in school who has good enough dresses to attend a proper tea. I think you'll find that asking her to stay dressed up is the only way she can come because like I said, she probably has nothing else. We'll use the fancy stuff and serve little biscuits with meat and cheese on them and we'll make tiny individual cakes for dessert. You'll see, she'll enjoy it and you may not be on her bad side if nothing else. You two can play with your dolls in your room. It'll just be a couple of hours, then she'll go home and you can practice your magic.

Ok mama, I'll ask, now I'm going to sleep, I'm so very tired.

When morning came, they both were excited about the day. Cassandra wanted to help Peter so much and she wanted to get it all over with Millie. She was sure she'd make a big joke out of going to tea with her.

Miranda fixed two sandwiches and sent a pint of milk for her and Peter to share. She sent pieces of cake and apples. When lunchtime rolled around, Peter was very excited to sit near

Cassandra because he was hoping she might like to trade her sandwich for his egg again. She was very happy to offer her trade. Mama sent us both a piece of cake and some milk if you'd like some. She was glad you were being so kind to me and trading and sharing lunches. She said to tell your mama to come visit her for lunch or dinner soon. She wants to thank her for raising such a wonderful son. You can come too if it's dinner.

Ok, I'll tell her, but she works a lot and doesn't have too many friends.

Tell her to please come. My mama is lonely and needs a friend she can talk to. We'll play with my marbles or something after dinner and let them talk. Tell her not to worry, my mama's real nice and will do her best to make you both comfortable. Is your daddy gone?

Yes, he left us a long time ago. I never really knew him. My mama has taken care of me all by herself. She works at the inn, cooking, and serving ale. She works long hours but we have each other.

Sounds like she might be lonely too and need a friend to talk to. Promise me you'll convince her to come and I'll bring you a cow. We have more cows now than stalls, so I have to get rid of one and I'd love for you to have it. Do you have a place to keep it?

We sure do! He exclaimed with eyes as wide as saucers. You really have one to get rid of? Can I work to buy it from you?

I don't want you to buy it. I want to know it has a good home. Someone who will feed it, milk it, and talk to it. Cows need company too. They get lonely, just like people. Didn't you know that? Peter shook his head and looked very thoughtfully at his feet. Thinking about lonely cows no doubt; or lonely boys and their mothers. He was a little quiet through the rest of their meal.

Well we're finished eating, so it's time to bite the bullet. I'll be right back. She hopped up and with much purpose in her step, headed over to Millie to invite her to tea. She hesitated at first but Cassandra kept talking until she'd gotten everything out about a fancy dress and all.

Ok, I would love to have tea with you and your mother on Saturday. I appreciate the opportunity to meet her and see your lovely home up close. I've admired it for a long time. It's so grand.

I don't know how long we'll be living there,

we're here to help a sick friend recover. Our house is not nearly so grand and it's a couple days away from here.

Miranda and Cassandra set about to get more details on those in the community who really needed some help. Peter and his mother did come to supper one night. They enjoyed a hearty dinner and Miranda told her about some of her struggles of being a single parent while the children went off to play marbles. LaDonna explained much of her life as well. She thanked her and then brought up the cow. "I know kids do and say things they don't always know is possible, or before they check with their parents, so I wanted to tell you that you are not responsible for the cow she promised Peter."

Oh no! She was serious and had been looking for someone she could trust to take her cow. We don't have enough stalls for them all and the young ones are getting too big to share now. She was worried that the cow would be slaughtered for food, or not talked to or taken care of properly. We'll bring several bales of hay for her when we bring her down and if you need more, just let me know. We have plenty and knowing you and Peter were taking good care of her would mean the world to us both. Do you have a churn to make some butter from the milk? I have several and could give you one of the small ones. I've got milk coming out my ears. I can't get it worked up fast enough.

Actually, I don't have one and that is very generous of you to loan it to me and to give us the cow. We will be very happy to have it and appreciative of the milk it provides for us in turn. You are very kind to give it to us.

I asked several of the ladies to come make apple products with me so I could get to know some of you, but I still have a lot of apples left too. If you'd like to take some of them, I'll get the children to help me gather everything and we'll bring it and the cow down tomorrow.

I appreciate your generosity, but I don't want you thinking we need the charity.

Oh, I would never want to insult you. Peter says you work hard to provide for him and I appreciate that. I make soap and perfumes from my flowers and sell them in the big cities to have money to take care of Cassandra and myself; so I know what hard work is as well.

That's so interesting, is it easy to make, the soap I mean? I have several flowers around the house and I might be able to make some too. Just for me and Peter of course, not to sell. I was just thinking it would be cheaper to make than to buy and he gets so dirty when he plays.

It is pretty easy, I can show you if you'd like. We could make a big batch together and then split it for the four of us to use. It's always easier to learn when you're doing it or being shown rather than just getting instructions. And I always appreciate a helping hand in anything I'm doing.

That sounds wonderful, just let me know what to bring and we can do it Sunday if that's ok with you.

Sunday is perfect for me. As I was saying, I know how hard it gets and I don't want to offend you, but like the cow, I have more than we can use and I absolutely hate to throw food away when someone can use it. It's a sin to be wasteful and I've been blessed with all this. We had two sets of twin calves born this past spring and more apples in our orchard than ever before. I'll have to butcher one of last year's steers soon and even with preserving much of it with salt, we won't be able to eat it all before it ruins. If you want some of that you can have it or if you feel you just can't use it before it ruins, then maybe you know some other family who can use it.

Well, if you really can't use it, we could take some. If you know someone else who could use it, please share with them as well. I just hate to take all your stuff.

Even if it means it will go to waste? Maybe you could earn it if that would make you feel better.

If I can, what do you have in mind?

Well I'm just horrible at cutting Cassandra's hair and mine is in bad need of some shears as well. Peter said you cut his and it's perfect. Maybe we could trade haircuts for beef?

Now that's a plan I can get on board with, but only if you're truly going to have more than you can use.

I do, and I'm not even going to be able to use all I have left from last year before I have to kill another, so if you could take some of that home with you. It would definitely make me feel better about not losing any of it too. We eat very well as our land supplies us plenty, but we can't eat that much! It's another reason we open the gates and invite the town folk in sometimes to help eat what we felt had to be cooked. You are probably always working and can't get here when we do that so we probably owe you some anyway. We gave away thirty-two chickens last week and we still are getting more eggs than we can use. Would you like a chicken or two as well?

She smiled, said that would be nice, and expressed her thanks for gaining such good friends for her and Peter.

Miranda and Cassandra stood arm in arm waving to their friends as they watched them go with food for both their lunches and suppers tomorrow.

Tomorrow, we gather stuff and deliver to Peter's house. So bring him home with you after school and I'll have a snack ready and then we'll load everything up and head into town. Before school though, I want to see if you can move an entire haystack onto the wagon without losing any. That's a good challenge for your magic homework, and if we do it before school, Peter won't be here to see it. I'll gather some of the apple products, some soap and perfume and we'll pick apples fresh tomorrow afternoon too. Oh you need to produce a few chickens too. I can't give them some if we're running short. It's hard enough to get them to take stuff I tell them is going to spoil. We're both getting haircuts this week too, when LaDonna comes to make soap with me. She's cutting our hair and we're giving her beef.

Now let's get to bed, we've a busy day tomorrow. We have to help our new friends and we have to bake some stuff for our tea on

Saturday. I think we definitely want some fancy little cakes. You know the kind we had at the party for the town. They're just about two bites each, but oh so tasty. We can send some home with Millie and you can take your teacher some too.

OH, that sounds really really good mama. I love cake!

I know dear, your sweet tooth is just about as big as mine!

Can I make strawberries dipped in chocolate too. I love those.

Absolutely dear. Tea is when you have special treats to share.

12 – Helping Others

The best magic is putting smiles on the faces of those who have little to smile about; and everyone can perform that kind. You don't have to be a witch to manage it; you just have to be kind, honest, and polite along with having a good giving heart. How's that for a good lesson to start the day with sleepy head?

It's good mama. I love helping people and especially when I get to do it personally. I can see what they need, help provide it, and I get to see the results. Ok, let's get that wagon loaded so I can have breakfast.

They both pulled on their boots and headed to the barn. Now stack 10 bales of hay on the front of the wagon and then you can put this big haystack in behind it.

Cassandra took a deep breath envisioned her task, spoke the words. **Powers of Earth and Sky, give me the powers this day to move this hay to help my friend. So mote it be done for me.** Less than a blink later, the hay was all moved, bales and stack at the same time without losing a single handful of hay. She looked over at her mother and took a bow. Miranda laughed and applauded her efforts.

Ok, let's get in for breakfast, you have to go to

school and I'll gather everything else, except the cow, chickens and the apples. You two can help with that after school.

Mama! You got up early and made biscuits! I love biscuits. Can I take some with jam for lunch?

Of course. I made enough for our breakfast and your and Peter's lunch too. I love them just as much as you do and I bet Peter does as well. Even if he's eating his egg each day, at least it will taste better with something different to go with it. I bet he's running a little faster these days, now that he's getting some proper nutrition to help his body grow and function as it should. He was probably too tired to run and play much with no fuel going in to replace what he used up.

He is doing more and smiling a lot more too mama. I am too! I like him and all my friends. It makes school seem more like playtime when you have so much fun there. I'm not having any trouble with my arithmetic any longer either. Ms. Catherine is such a good teacher. She's so patient with all of us.

Ok, off to school with you. I've got a busy day. There's washing to do as well.

Miranda decided to use magic to do the

laundry. She just made it clean and folded without the washing and drying. That always took all day. She wanted to be fresh to do the hauling and unloading at Peter's and maybe they'd see if the grass needed cutting or the flowers weeded. Maybe something needed mending when they got there. LaDonna never got home before dark and it sure was hard to work on stuff in the dark. She had all sorts of plans in mind for when the children got home.

In the meantime, however, she gathered jars and jugs full of apple butter, cider, juice, flour, meal, lard, onions, garlic, salt, butter, eggs, milk and potatoes. From the pantry she retrieved about thirty pounds of salted pork and beef, candles, lamp oil, soap, perfume and some cleaning products. She would have gotten more, but figured LaDonna would be offended if she way overdid it. She had found some sacks in the barn and filled six of them with corn to help feed the cow and chickens. She gathered some seeds for them to plant Peter a garden. There would be potatoes, corn, tomatoes, cucumbers and peppers. That should help give them enough variety of vegetables to cook with and have side dishes with the meat they'd be getting in the fall after slaughter and harvest time. Oh, and she almost forgot the churn. LaDonna had already accepted that gift, so she didn't want to forget it. They would need and love some fresh butter.

She was ready when the children got home. She'd even gathered the apples so they'd have more time to work at Peter's house. She packed them some meat, cheese, bread, and milk so they could eat on the way into town. They needed to save as much daylight as they could. They were going to be very busy and they would be tired as well.

When they started out with the wagon, the cow was tied to the back, so they had to go slowly, and the chickens were perched on top of the haystack. They seemed to enjoy the view. By the time they'd reached Peter's small house, the chickens were in the children's arms being petted.

When they arrived, the first thing they had to do was unload the food. Once that was finished they looked at the place where the cow would be kept. It was a small shelter with one stall, probably meant for a horse, but would work nicely. There were two sections, the smaller one would work nicely for the chickens. One side of it was sorely in need of repair. Miranda sent Peter to get the hammer and nails from the wagon seat and she and Cassandra would look for some boards they might be able to use. Well of course there were boards, Cassandra provided them with a wink at her mother. They were even nicely weathered like the shed. Miranda had provided the nails and tools with her magic. When Peter returned they were ready to fix the shed.

Looks like the boards were just knocked loose, so a few nails and this board for support nailed crosswise and I'll have this shed fixed Peter. You want to hold the boards while I hammer? He was very pleased to be of help and they had it fixed in a matter of minutes. It took both children to pick up the bales of hay and stack them in the section with the chickens. There was just enough room for them to the right of the nests they built from a couple wooden boxes laying just inside the door. They cleared some vines and weeds that were holding the door open and you'd think they'd created a palace by the way Peter was beaming when he showed Miranda their efforts.

Now, the haystack and we'll have everything unloaded. Cassandra, were there any more boards laying around? I'm thinking we could build an overhang from the roof to put the haystack under and keep it fresher for the cow. Sure is mama. Looks like there might have been another room or lean-to on the side of this shed. She came back around the side carrying some perfectly sized boards for the job. Once they fixed a roof, they unloaded the hay. They couldn't get the trailer real close, but they all took turns pitching hay until it was stacked nicely under the new roof.

Peter, we've got about two hours left till dark, would you like to raise a garden over there. It looks like someone has in the past.

Would I? You're not joking are you? I'd love a garden, so would mama. Do you have seeds? We've got a couple hoes we could dig up the soil with.

I have seeds, so let's get started. They took turns and Cassandra used her magic to make every stroke of the hoes do the work of ten strokes. It still took the entire two hours, but they had planted a nice little garden. It would provide a lot of food for the two of them, and Peter was so proud that he would be able to help with food.

I'll be sure and talk to the cow every day Cassandra. I don't want you to worry at all. She'll be loved and I'll protect her and make sure she has food and water all the time.

That's great! And she'll provide you with milk, cream and butter. I love butter! Especially on a biscuit, don't you?

Saturday came and so did Millie. She had her

best dress on and so did Cassandra. Miranda had set the table with the best dishes and had a lovely spread of food on the table. Everything was so delicate and dainty looking. They even had flowers on the table. It was really fancy and the three of them sure looked the part of royalty.

We're so glad you were able to come to tea Millie. Cassandra has told me so much about you.

Ms. Miranda, about that, I'm not sure what all Cassandra has told you, but I want you to know, that a lot of the time, I'm not a very nice girl. I've been nice to her, but not so nice to a lot of the other children at school. I'm ashamed of myself really. But I never cared until I met your daughter. She has shown kindness to every child she's met at school, even the most despicable one, me. I'm no better than any other child there, but I act like I am. I try to act so important and like my family is the best in town. Truth is, ma'am, my papa has practically nothing to his name. We live in a house provided by the town and his pay is from taxes paid by all the town folk. As, I'm sure you've noticed, it's not a rich place and there are not a lot of taxes paid, so we don't get a lot of pay. My papa is a proud man and well, my mama broke his will when she up and left us. He loved her so much, but she didn't like being poor and when some man came through town and offered to take her away, well she went. She left him and me behind. I was just starting to walk and talk when she left and I don't remember her really at all.

That's such a shame Millie. Sometimes people get so low they just don't know how to cope any longer. I'm sure she didn't really want to leave either of you. She probably just felt trapped and didn't know what to do. Your papa loves you very much and is doing what he can, but as you said, he's broken and just doesn't know how to get out of his situation. Maybe we can do something about that as well.

Papa said we should act like nothing happened and people would soon forget she ever left. When I started school and children would ask about her. I would drop my eyes and tell them she was gone. I sometimes even cried. I knew they would think she was dead and that was my hope. It was easier than telling folks that she didn't love me enough to stay. We get by with enough to eat, but I only have two dresses to my name and they're getting pretty worn. My nightshirt has more holes in it than it has material and I can't play with the others at school because if I tear my dress, I'll have nothing to wear to school. I only accepted your offer of tea today, because I knew I would have food to eat and I could eat until my stomach was full and I've not done that in a long time. I hope you will forgive me for my meanness and still let me stay for tea today. I just had to tell you because I couldn't take advantage of your generosity any longer without telling you the truth. I just feel too bad about how I've been and Cassandra didn't show me pity, she showed me friendship and I'll forever be grateful to both of you for that.

Miranda reached for her and pulled her close as she began wiping the tears away. I think you are a very courageous girl to have lived this way so long and not have broken down. I think you do need to change and be nice to others and there may be some that would help you in return. I know for a fact that Cassandra has a trunk full of old clothes in her room that no longer fit her and I think she's just about a size bigger than you. Let's have our tea and then we'll see how many of those things will work for you. Then maybe you can fit in with all the rest of the children at school and actually get to play and enjoy life a little. It's what children are supposed to do.

Their tea was truly lovely and of course there was a trunk full of clothes in just Millie's size. Cassandra saw to that. One and only one fancy dress, but there were many others that would be most suitable for school and playing.

There were ten in all, along with shoes, bonnets, under things and night shirts too.

Miranda also put some blankets, and bed linens in a box with some towels and aprons too. Millie cried again and again and thanked them over and over. We've been cleaning out our pantry as well and discovered we have an abundance of food that won't last another year so we've been giving a lot away as our harvest looks good and we should have plenty to keep us through the winter. We'll pack a lot of that up for you as well. If your papa asks, you just tell him it's all paid for. You've gotten a job. You're going to be tutoring some of the younger children at school who are having difficulties.

I actually would love to do that. I've wanted to be a teacher for such a long time. Ms. Catherine is so good at it. She makes it all easy to understand and is so patient with all of us. I love her!

Then it's settled! Now mama, we'd better load the wagon and take Millie home.

We will, if she'll promise to come have tea with us and help you play with your dolls whenever you both want. AGREED! they both shouted.

13 – Helping the World

They had taken a lot of time away from her magic studies to do good for many in the community and there was nothing wrong with that, but they needed to get back to it; three years would be gone before they knew it. The rest of the coven had gone back to their homes a couple weeks ago. Lorissa was back to her normal self and there was no need for them to continue to stay and not return to their normal lives.

Cassandra, I'm going to have to go back and check on the house. I'll only be gone a week or less. Do you want to go with me or stay here with Lorissa?

If you think she'll be ok by herself and it won't be dangerous to leave her alone, I'd like to go with you. Since we have a small wagon and horses too, maybe we could travel a little slower and spend a night under the stars.

I'd like that dear. We'll also do some magic along the way and actually start with some spells to produce a new wagon and horses. That would be a good way to get things moving along. You've already learned you don't need anything to make something. Your magic can do that alone, but let's say you had someone who you wanted to turn into a horse, or a bug for instance, then you'll need to learn how to change a horse into a man and a man into a horse. It's easier to use magic when you're scared, but if you're too scared, you won't think correctly or in time; so you have to practice ahead. These type spells come in handy if you have a dragon flying at you, breathing fire and you need to escape. You can turn him into a fly.

A dragon? Really there are dragons too? I've always wanted to see a dragon. Are there ones that don't breathe fire? Because that could get pretty dangerous, even for an accomplished witch I'd think. I can't believe they are real. I always thought they were part of the fairytales you told me.

Don't you remember I also told you that everything was true. None of the stories were fairytales. To answer your question: Yes, young dragons cannot breathe fire. That comes with maturity. Now back to the lesson. If there is a man chasing you, you can turn him into a bug. If you have to carry a load a long distance and you don't want people to know you're a witch, then you turn a frog into a man to help you, or rabbits into horses to pull a wagon. I want you to find things in the courtyard or garden to turn into a horse and wagon. We shouldn't need anything bigger than that for the trip. I'll be out in about twenty minutes to see what you have come up with. I'll have our clothes packed and we'll be ready to go then. Say goodbye to Lorissa on your way to the courtyard.

Ok mama, I'll see you in just a few minutes.

Miranda left the room, but went straight to a window to watch what Cassandra was doing. There seemed to be absolutely no animals around and she was looking in lots of places where they might be. Finally she decided to try a trick she knew. She produced an apple and then smashed it against a rock. It broke apart and juice ran out on the ground. She sat patiently watching the apple and it was barely three minutes before she had her supplies. An ant had come out of the grass to gather some apple bits to take back to its home. She spoke her spell and watched in delight as the ant grew into a beautiful horse. She still watched the apple and was soon rewarded with a gnat that landed on the spilled juice and began drinking. She used her magic, speaking her spell and turned the gnat into a very ornate wagon.

Miranda waved her arms and a carpet bag appeared along with a picnic basket. She picked them up and headed out to the courtyard. I'm all packed.

What do you think of the wagon mama, I'm just

about ready to hitch the horse to it.

It's very impressive, why do we have such a fancy one?

We'll it wasn't really my intention, but when I turned the gnat into it, its wings turned an odd way and its head and horn, or whatever that thing is it drinks with spread apart and flattened out. Anyway, it looks like someone spent a lot of time carving a wagon out of a giant tree as it's all one piece. I wasn't intending to do that, but don't you think it's beautiful?

I do and I think you did it whether intentionally or not. I think you are creative and it shows in everything you do. I bet that ant is wondering how in the world it got so big and why it had gotten so furry. Cassandra giggled and finished her spell to produce the rigging to hitch the horse and carriage together for their journey.

Miranda put the bags in the wagon and climbed up top. You want to drive?

Sure mama. I'd love to, at least for a while.

Good, I'll watch for things you can use your magic on. Oh, like the gates, open them with magic and close them behind us. Then head to Peter's house. We'll let him know we're going to be gone about a week and he can tell your teacher too. After that, you'll need to head southeast for the rest of the day.

When Cassandra had spoken with Peter and assured him they would be back in a week, they were not going away forever, she climbed back on the wagon, and looked at her mother and asked "How do I know what direction is southeast?"

Ah, you need to look at the sun and determine your direction.

Well it rises in the east and sets in the west so that direction is east and south is always to the right of east if you're looking east; so I should go midway between east and south.

Very good. Now whatever animal should happen to cross our path, I want you to turn it into a butterfly. Just keep your eyes open until you see something.

What if the first thing I see is already a butterfly?

Then make it a flower. I don't think that will be an issue, but I know, you're just being prepared. It wasn't too long before a rabbit hopped into the field in front of them. Quick as a blink he was floating on air flapping his butterfly wings. Cassandra was good at these skills and fast too. There was no hesitation in her; but she needed to be tested if something were vicious and maybe looking to turn her into something like dinner. So Miranda made a wolf appear. When he saw them, he leaped from the rock he was standing on. He was near but above their heads and before he could clear the rock with his hind feet, Cassandra had turned him into a rabbit and she caught him in her arms when he had jumped. She petted him between the ears and asked if they wanted rabbit stew for dinner. Miranda smiled and told her she didn't; so she let him go. Miranda turned him back into a wolf and he ran the opposite direction that they were going. They both laughed till their sides ached.

I'm so proud of you sweetheart, you didn't let fear guide you. You just did what needed done, in a blink, and you didn't have to think about what to do or hesitate at all. You have to be that fast or you'll be dead; or worse, you could be the one in the spell. You can fight magic, but you have to be fast in your mind and on your feet. Now I believe I'm getting hungry; are you ready to stop for lunch?

I am. What did you pack for lunch?

Why I didn't pack anything. I guess you're going to have to imagine some food and make it for us. Do you have any ideas? Oh, and before you start naming your favorites, I'd like you to think of something you don't like as much as other things, then think of a way to make it better and we'll have that. I'll give the horse some apples and tie him in the shade of that tree for a bit so he can rest too.

That's hard. Let me think a minute. You know I love chicken, but I don't like turkey as much. So let's try turkey. Now to make it better...maybe we could stuff it in a roll with vegetables and gravy or cheese. Cheese makes just about everything better.

I think you're on to something. Why don't we stuff turkey, spinach, tomatoes, cucumber and onions in a roll. I don't think the gravy and cheese would be very good together. Then we can add cheese with peas and have with it, not really a soup, but sort of.

That sounds like a very good lunch mama. Here we go.

Oh, the rolls look so good, mama. I think I'll dip mine in my cheese and peas as I eat. This is wonderful. We should think up stuff more often! They both ate every bite and used their bread to sop up the very last of the cheese in their bowls as well.

Let's get on the road and think about dessert for a while and see what we can come up with for that. Something new and different, remember. They were both just quietly enjoying the sunshine and the occasional animal or bird that passed by when suddenly in front of them appeared a large table and chairs with a tent over it. Cassandra looked over at her mother rather sheepishly and said. I guess I thought about it too hard. I didn't speak a spell or anything, I just thought about dessert and once I'd concocted it in my head, it sounded so good I thought I can't wait to stop and fix that; and it was there, right in front of us.

Cassandra, you are going to have to be extremely careful, you are becoming very powerful. That shouldn't have happened without you speaking a spell aloud, or in your mind at least. When the mere thought of something in your head becomes reality, you could cause serious problems. You'll have to work on focusing and keeping your thoughts light so your magic doesn't kick in due to your subconscious mind doing the spell.

I will mama. Do you think the emotion I felt with it was the cause?

Maybe

I'll be extra careful any time I'm excited, anxious, or especially if I become angry.

That's a good plan dear, now let's go see what you've created for our dessert and have a bite of whatever it is that couldn't wait.

Ok, she said as she hopped down, it has all my favorite things put together. There is a brownie on the bottom with soft peanut butter candy on top of that. Then a cookie with chocolate pieces inside and that's covered with strongly beaten sweetened cream for the next layer. Then there is strawberries, blueberries and raspberries on top of that and for the finale there is chocolate syrup striped all over the top.

Now that does sound good. I think I may just like your thinking child. Let's dig in! One bite and together they said MMM with their eyes closed and then they laughed. Why was it not just on a table, or in my hands? What made you feel the need for a tent and big table?

It was just too grand for anything small, and remember I didn't choose it, my mind did. I will be careful as I can be mama. I don't want anything bad to happen with my magic. I always want to do good with it. I want to be just like you and Lorrissa, Parisa, Seraphina, Ariel Evangeline, Laila and Melek too. Are we ready to move on now, or are we staying here under this beautiful tent for the night? I could make the table disappear and leave the tent. We can pull the wagon under it and make our beds in the wagon. Might be more comfortable than the ground. Of course, though, I could make it extremely comfortable with some mattresses, pillows and soft blankets. I see the look. Did I go too far?

Maybe just a bit, but the blankets, tent, pillows and wagon sound pretty good. It seems like it's going to be too warm for a fire since we'll be off the ground and under some soft fancy blankets. It will be a good opportunity for me to teach you the spell of boundaries. It sort of puts you inside a bubble, but only the person doing the spell can get out or let the person out they put in the bubble.

Oh that sounds like fun. We'll be safe and secure in our own little world. Can the people outside the bubble see the people inside or are they protected at an even higher level?

It's higher. Unless they are a witch or warlock themselves, a fae, or some other creature that holds magic, then they don't even know, it or whatever it's protecting, is even there.

Will you tell me stories about when you were learning magic while we wait till bedtime? Maybe we can dream up another magically good tasting meal for dinner.

Let's work on that first, then after dinner you

can amaze me with your talents at decorating with all your fancy pillows and blankets. I think I want to have fish for dinner. Can you think of something wonderful to do with fish?

Hmm, let me think. I like several kind of fish, so I have to think about what spices would go with each kind and what side dish I might make. Oh, I've got it. I hope you're ready, because dinner is about to be served. Please be seated so dinner may commence.

As they sat, plates, silverware, glasses filled with punch and domed plates appeared. When Cassandra lifted the domes, they had salmon cakes, fried perfectly, fried potatoes, fried squash, sliced deep red tomatoes, and yeast rolls. Miranda could only smile as each bite passed her pallet. When they'd finished eating, Cassandra announced as though she'd never stopped talking from the beginning.

And for dessert, we have chocolate covered nuts. I've made a whole assortment. There are peanuts, cashews, almonds, brazil nuts and macadamia nuts. I double dipped them all.

Perfect! Was all Miranda had to say. Then she began telling Cassandra of the mishaps she had made while learning her magic. She told of spills, smoke, explosions and all sorts of animals that don't really exist. She explained she had a hard time focusing, so instead of a goat, she might make a sheep/goat combination. It had a goat's head and the body of a sheep, all covered in thick wool and it sounded like a sick sheep when it made a sound. Of course she was much younger when she began her lessons, but still she didn't think she was or ever would be as strong as it seemed Cassandra was going to be.

Now that storytelling is done for the night, here is what you need to do. First make our blankets and pillows then call on the powers of the earth, sky and wind to come together as one and give you power to wield an invisible shield, then you have to see yourself bending and folding the shield so that it surrounds us both; then seal the circle with your magic so it cannot be broken by any other, within or without so long as you live, or release the shield yourself.

She did as she was told; calling on all the powers of the earth with an authority that seemed second nature to her. Authority that most witches her age would be too timid to claim. Miranda would never be in danger if her daughter were around. She had the power and she was quickly learning how to use it to its full effect. This also worried Miranda some, for she feared as her power grew, that Zythora's knowledge of her would increase and she might call out to those watching over her to try to destroy Cassandra or to take her captive and isolate her so she doesn't perform magic. She may even poison her to the point of dying; as she just may be the only witch alive that can rid them all of Zythora and that should make her very anxious, especially since Cassandra hadn't even fully come into her powers yet.

Mama, I did it! It's like a glass jar all around us. We can see out, we are warm and protected and no one can see in, right?

That's correct. Even if they come in contact with our bubble, they can't see us. They would walk right over and not even notice that there was a bump in their way. The magic won't let them see us or anything else in the bubble either. It's a great way to protect something or someone you care about and it's very strong, as strong as your powers are. Another thing, if you are not inside and would be killed, the shield is still in effect. Unless the spell is cast to release upon your death, it can never be opened. So you should remember to make that part of your spell should you be protecting me, Peter, or someone else you love. Even if you have possessions you would want someone to have upon your death, if you don't speak that into the spell, no one will ever be able to find it or get inside to get the stuff you wanted them to have. The spell should indicate who you want to have the stuff and have the magic take it to them wherever they are at your death. I think that it will be many years before your death, but it's something for you to know. Oh Cassandra, I just had the greatest epiphany!

What's an epippany mama?

It's an illuminating discovery. And my discovery is about Zythora. I propose we put her in a bubble. A shield that's folded into a box or round circle. She's already cursed to a chained up box buried in the center of Drenidore, but if we or you, put a bubble around all that, then even those looking for her would not be able to see where to find her. It's one more safeguard for us to keep her contained until she's destroyed. I believe Drenidore is too big now to put a bubble around it, but one just around Zythora and her box, would work. It would even prevent someone unknowingly opening the box or undoing the chains. Humans are a nosey bunch of people and if they are challenged, they rise to the occasion and take it very personally. Most of them will do it or die trying, if given a challenge. It's been the fall of many great men and woman. I'll give you my strength too to get the bubble completed. We'll take a day to rest before we attempt it after we reach home late tomorrow.

I'm glad you had the epipanny mama. I think we can do it and I love working with you, whether it's in the garden, the kitchen or doing magic. I learn so much.

Epiphany, dear, and I'm glad you enjoy it because I sure have been having fun teaching you the skills you'll need to do your job as a witch. Whether it be banishing an evil witch or destroying her. I know with just a little help, you can do anything you wish to do.

Now, let's get to sleep in our nice bubble bed.

Cassandra giggled and leaned over for her kiss good-night.

14 - The Journey Home

They slept like babies and got up early and had biscuits with molasses for breakfast and were on their way home. They hadn't been there in months so they both were looking forward to seeing their stuff and their little home that was all theirs.

As the house came into view, they both sighed and smiled. The field was tall with grass, but the sky was blue and they felt the peace inside that they were home. It was theirs and nearly all their memories revolved around that house. Until this trip, Cassandra had never been anywhere but that house. She was born there and it was all she knew until the day she discovered she was a witch. Then her whole world began to open up. She knew things and saw things she'd only thought were fairy tales before. She had experienced more in the last month than in her entire life. She was growing mentally and maturing at a rapid rate. The little girl would be leaving within the year and a young lady would be developing. It was nearly a lifetime of change for her, but it was good and Miranda would see her through every step of it.

They were probably not home for more than an hour before they heard the familiar sound of a wolf howling. They looked at each other, smiled and put down whatever they had in their hands and headed for the forest. They were much closer to Javen, but Angelica arrived to meet them all at the same time. She'd heard his call and knew they were home.

After the pleasantries of welcoming them back and how good it was for everyone to see everyone, they got down to business. Angelica explained their concerns and Miranda explained her epiphany on the journey there. They all agreed it needed to be done and at the earliest possible moment. Javen knew where the center of the forest was and he would go there so Cassandra would have a better vision of where her powers would need to be directed, so no chance would be taken and no power expended unnecessarily. He could also get close enough to make sure the bubble took as it would be visible to him while it was being applied. They felt a little relief that the hold on Zythora would be a little stronger. None of them felt safe as long as she lived.

They had enough strength to tighten her bonds. But they would still have to grow stronger, especially Cassandra, and wait for her 16th birthday, in order to destroy her once and for all.

Miranda sent mental messages to the white witches to come and help them be strong enough to place this bubble around Zythora. They wanted to do it in two days, that would give them enough time to leisurely travel there, thus avoiding any sense of urgency, and this should keep anyone helping Zythora from finding out and trying to stop them. They wanted everything to look normal and like every other day. Any attention drawn here would cause a lot of suspicion and unwanted company. She had Cassandra send a message to Lorissa so she'd be extra careful since they would all be farther away from her should she need protection. Lorissa's daughter, Sarina, was still in hiding and they didn't want a repeat of her last meeting with Lorissa, or something worse if she had her way. Lorissa had placed security fields around her castle. It required a password for anyone to enter, so only those given the code could enter unless Lorissa allowed them entrance. They all felt better about leaving her alone there once this was in place.

Cassandra went close to the forest to practice her magic so Javan could watch her. Should anything go awry then he could howl and Miranda would come running. He really loved watching her make things disappear and reappear. She told him her biggest secret. Even her mother didn't know and she couldn't tell her yet, but she wanted a dragon. One to love and train to be not just her pet, but her helper. She wanted to teach it how to hunt and destroy as well as to be kind and gentle. She knew it would take some time, but she had a few years to work with it so she was going to start and when she felt they had built a good relationship, she'd tell her mother. Javan cautioned her to consider everything about a dragon first. Make sure she had a good hiding place for it, plenty of food for it to eat and shelter from the elements and any humans who may seek to destroy it. They tend to act first and ask questions after it's too late, he explained. People automatically assume that dragons are bad and just want to eat or destroy them.

I'll be careful, but I want one so badly I have to concentrate a lot to keep my mind from just making one appear. Another reason I've not told mama. I'm afraid the more I talk about it and think about it the more control I'll lose. Do you think I could make a tiny one that I could keep under my bed during the beginning and then make him grow into an amazing creature as his training progressed? He would be trained to do good.

I don't know, but I do know that you need to tell your mother before you have one very long. She'll not be excited to find something on fire one morning and it be you in your bed because the dragon lost control while you were asleep.

Good point. I'll talk to her about it very soon. I mean she was the one to bring dragons up. I didn't know they were even real.

I wish you could come inside Drenidore, we have some of the most amazing creatures living in our forest. Once the curse is lifted, they'll...um, we'll all be able to use our magic again and this place will come alive with light and color. The flowers will once again have vibrant hues and the trees will give way to the sunshine. It was beautiful before the curse, and the creatures were full of life, love and energy. It was a happy place with everyone doing their part to make it wonderful.

I look forward to seeing it. First stop Zythora, second stop Drenidore. Do you think I can do this bubble thing?

I sure do Cassandra, you are an amazing girl. I think you can do anything you put your mind to. Plus, you're going to have your coven helping you. You can't help but do this.

Thanks! Well I'd better go see if mama has anything for me to do. See you later!

Javan watched as his friend walked home. He knew one thing for sure, his new friend had already changed his life. She'd brought hope where he'd almost lost all he ever had. He was sure she could do this. He'd seen her at work and she was fearless.

Mama!

I'm in here child. Have you tired of magic for the day or are you just ready for lunch?

Lunch! What are we having?

Whatever you imagine and make for us.

I think we'll have a nice potato soup, then some chopped chicken sandwiches and a frozen sweetened cream dessert with strawberries and chocolate bits mixed in.

Oooh, that sounds delicious! I've never tried frozen sweetened cream. What made you think of that?

I don't know mama, I just like to drink sweetened cream and it's hot out today, so if it were really really cold, it would have to be even better.

I think you're right, now make it all happen.

She did, each course in turn, with all the table trimmings, cutlery, and dishes. Even some pretty flowers in the middle of their table.

My, you think of everything Miranda praised her as she took a spoonful of the soup. And this is delicious too! Thank you, darling, for our lunch.

You're welcome mama. I like it too. They continued enjoying their meal through each course and finished with the ever so tasty frozen concoction.

Mama, if I do good on my chores and with my magic and the bubble, do you think I could have a pet of my own to take care of.

I think we can arrange that. Most witches have a familiar or a companion animal that protects them and helps them with their magic and deeds they want to do. Most witches find cats the easiest to work with and they love the power they get out of it too. They already think they're superior to everything else on the planet. Do you have one in mind?

Actually I do, but I think you'll think I'm silly and won't let me have it.

If you do good and show me you're responsible enough to care for it, then you can have whatever animal you choose.

REALLY!? I mean, really any animal I want?

Yes, dear. Now tell me what you want.

I want a dragon.

WHAT?!

Yes, mama, I want a dragon. I've been thinking about one ever since you mentioned it on the way here. I've already thought about everything it will need and how I'll have to take care of it. So...yes to a dragon?

Well I did say whatever you choose, but we'll have to work together to make sure you can contain it and keep it safe as well as the rest of the world. Do you want a male or female?

I hadn't thought about that. Have you had experience with either?

No I have not. I've only seen a couple dragons and I wasn't around them very long. But I do think the most powerful witch on the planet should have the most powerful familiar to accompany her; and I do think you're going to be the most powerful witch born to date. That's another reason why it's so important that you only use your powers for good. Remember that always. Temptations will come, like when you wanted to smack Millie. You have to overcome them at all costs.

I know mama, and I will too, not because it's the right thing to do, it's because that's who I am deep inside. I want to help others.

Ok, tell me more about this dragon. Are you going to make it with magic? Colors? Male or female? Where are you going to keep it? What's its name? How do you plan on training it? Will it be a baby or full grown?

I don't know all that, I've just been thinking about wanting one. I think I can make a cave in that half mountain at the palace for it to live. I know I can make enough cattle to keep it fed. I think I want a male, but I want him to have pretty colors, maybe teal metallic looking undersides to his wings, with mainly a darker blue for the main color, and a gray underbelly. He will have golden eyes, and magnificent horns lifting in a surreal beauty from his head, almost like a crown when he flares them out. I want him small to begin with for training and I'll enlarge him as we progress. Or he may just grow on his own at an acceptable rate to continue to train him. I think that when he's gained his fire, I want designs to appear in his armor that gently glow as his fire builds to a crescendo just before he lets it out.

He sounds beautiful. If you keep him small early on, the training will be much easier I think. That was smart of you. He'll need a powerful name.

I know, I just haven't thought of one yet. As soon as I do, I'll create him, but I want him to have a name from the beginning so he'll know I know him and he can know me.

That's a good idea.

Wait, I've got it! Greargon, Champion of the Skies. That sounds majestic and powerful don't you think?

I do and Cassandra you can make him right after we do the bubble and you rest for a day. No arguments or you can rest two days first.

That's great mama! I can't wait to hold him. It will be so cool and then later, he'll be holding me! I can see us now flying high as he carries me above the clouds on his back! Whew, what fun we'll have. Ok, I've got to stop or I won't be able to control myself. It's hard sometimes.

You're doing great and as you get stronger, it will be easier to control too. Why don't you go back near the forest so Javan can have some company. I think he likes to watch you do your magic. Just don't do anything too big, you need to conserve your strength for tomorrow. We'll be placing the bubble for a stronger hold on Zythora. Think about dinner while you're there and surprise me with something amazing.

I'll be doing laundry and cleaning house. Oh I have some mending to do as well. You don't have anything that needs taken care of do you?

No mama, but why are you mending, even by magic, when you can just make new with magic? I'm aware now and using, so you should take a break and do it all by magic.

I like to keep in shape and housework will do it for you. I don't want to get rusty on my skills as I may have to do it without magic. As soon as we can break the curse, we'll all live better lives, magic will once again be abundant in both our kingdoms. You will be queen one day and I will be old and worn. It will be wonderful to have things restored to the way they once were with everyone happy and life better for all. When we go back home, we'll try to do even more for our town folk so they can have better lives, I don't want them to be dependent on us, but I want them to have more. It's sometimes just a matter of having a deer in the right place when the men go hunting, or the garden producing an abundance of vegetables so there's plenty through the winter. They don't have to know we're using magic, but they'll know life is better.

I understand mama. I'm off now to make magic!

Javan was waiting for her. He was in a very good mood and had been since they'd returned. It must be very depressing in Drenidore. Miranda and Cassandra both wished they could make that better for all the residents, but it couldn't be done before Cassandra's 16th birthday. They would just have to give them as much diversion as they could while they were home. Especially since their new home was going to be in Lorissa's palace for the rest of Miranda's life anyway. She had decided that Cassandra needed the companionship and interaction with other children and adults; so she could learn different social skills from what she used with her mother. She needed to be a happy little girl as much as possible considering she would be carrying the weight of the world with her. They would be close to Lorissa and could protect her should Sarina decide to try anything else. This trip was so they could secure their personal belongings and mementos to take back with them. They may not be back for quite a while and that saddened them both quite a bit.

Miranda started gathering things to take to their new home. Some personal stuff and things her mother had given her; like her first wand. Hmmm, maybe she'd give that to Cassandra to begin with. She didn't know why they even used wands, other than to intimidate others. They didn't need them. A spell was a spell, whether a stick of some sort were pointed at a particular spot or not wouldn't matter in the scheme of things if the spell were spoken correctly. It was a witch thing though, so she supposed Cassandra would need one for appearances. Maybe it helped the witch focus more. No, she didn't need it for that and any good witch wouldn't either. Oh, that would explain it, it was needed for training, then it was just a memento or something to pass down to your little witch or warlock. She did have a lot of good memories from waving that wand in the air, and a few times she'd gotten in trouble too. Like when she'd changed Alexandria's hair color, or turned Timothy into a frog. She laughed out loud at the thought of the look on his face when his body became a frog. It was one of her early failed attempts. She'd had a lot of failed attempts, quite unlike Cassandra.

She contemplated whether it was the fact that she was older when she began training or if Cassandra was just a much stronger witch than herself. Either way she was glad her daughter would be stronger and more powerful than she was. She also knew that she was more ready to handle the pressures since she was older.

She wondered if it were really better to have withheld magic from her, or if she'd already be powerful enough to destroy Zythora had she lived with magic from the beginning. No need mulling it over now. It was moot. The deed was done, so good or bad there was no changing it now. She did smile though knowing that her daughter would be able to do anything she wanted to with her powers and she was confident that Cassandra would not be swayed to stray from her teaching that they were good witches and always practiced their magic for good and worked to destroy evil.

Her thoughts then turned to Cassandra's desire for a dragon as her familiar. It might be a rough training period. A cat may make a mess by not using the paper, but a dragon, now that's a real mess if it didn't go where it was supposed to. There was always a chain, but Miranda didn't like the thoughts of chaining up such a magnificent creature with human intelligence. They would just have to reason with it and show it their powers so it would know who the boss really was.

She was going to have to dig out the spell books to continue training as Cassandra had sped through all the basic stuff and they still had three years of training to go!

She knew they would work together to continue their work with the town folk once they'd gotten home, but it may just take a dragon to keep Cassandra occupied for the long three years they were facing before they could put an end to the curse and restore people's lives to them.

She finished gathering and sorting all her stuff to take home with her just as Cassandra returned to talk about dinner. She'd decided what to have and what to do after dinner that evening. Let me interrupt you for a minute. I've just located one of my prized possessions and I want you to have it. You can use it tomorrow. I think it will be the perfect accessory for any outfit. She pulled the wand from the box and presented it to her and then she set the box in the corner behind the door, ready for loading.

Mama! I love it! My very first wand!

It was my first wand too, actually my only wand. After finishing training, I've never used it again.

They moved to the kitchen and Miranda sat down to dinner. Cassandra prepared some of the most incredible little pies for them to have for appetizers, they were filled with eggs, onions, and bacon. Then for their main meal, they had pies again, filled with lamb and vegetables bathed in some very rich and hearty gravy. Then dessert was pie again. Made of a thick chocolate pudding that was mixed with light airy whipped cream so the whole thing was light and fluffy when they took a bite. She'd shaved chocolate over the top so it was very pretty as well as just a little richer too.

As soon as they'd finished eating, Cassandra twirled around in the middle of the kitchen and everything was cleaned, put away and in order, just exactly where it was supposed to be. Now for a magic game mama. I think you should make lighted bugs and I'll catch them. We'll stay on the porch swing and make them way over in the field and I'll pop them into this jar. She held up a gallon jar and beamed a smile at her mother.

Now how do I know you won't cheat and just make new ones appear in this jar?

Mama! First of all, I don't cheat, secondly, I've already thought of that, you will make each one a different color. If you make blue, I'll make it pop in my jar and you can look to see if I caught a blue one or not, plus you'll be watching to see if yours disappears.

Cassandra, can you imagine how beautiful that jar full of lighted bugs will be when it's full of every color in the world glowing at the same time in that small space!

I can. It should be a sight to behold. I think it's dark enough for them to show up in the distance, so let's get started. Alright mama:

On your mark, get set, GO!

They spent over an hour catching those lighted bugs, laughing, talking and just being little girls with no care in the world. Not even beginning to think about the evil lurking so close to them in Drenidore. But that was for tomorrow, tonight they were cheerful and happy, tomorrow they could carry the weight of the world on their shoulders and accomplish what needs to be.

They went inside as the chill became obvious in the air. It was nearly bedtime.

We'd better get to bed as the others will be here early in the morning and we have to be rested to take on the task of strengthening our hold over Zythora.

Oh, mama. I'll dream of breakfast for everyone and have it right after they arrive, so you won't have to worry with that in the morning. I'll make some special treats so they can have whatever they may want.

That sounds like a very good plan sweetheart.

I love you very much. Good night.

Good night mama.

15 – First Contact

The order arrived just after daybreak and Cassandra took about two minutes to produce a spread fit for a king. She made everything she'd ever eaten for breakfast and everything she'd heard talked about and whipped up a couple combinations that she'd never heard of; but she figured if it had pancakes, meat and something sweet, or eggs, meat and a savory sauce, then it couldn't be bad. They were all impressed with the banquet she'd prepared.

Witches had an impressive appetite and if they were not careful, they became very plump. It seems that might be where the humans got the idea that some of them ate children. Regardless of where they got the notion, it sure worked in scaring the children. They were very careful to avoid witches and would usually go screaming to their mommies if they saw one.

Albeit they were not truly in contact with Zythora, they knew she was very aware of their presence near the forest. She would have to feel the power generating with all those witches so close together and so close to her. She wondered what was up, but there was not a lot she could do to stop them, no matter what they were cooking up. She'd just have to wait and see what happened and she didn't like waiting on anyone else or not knowing. She definitely didn't like not being in charge of what was happening. She might have been able to glean some of their power, but if she did, her curse on the forest would just drain that magic from her, so there was no point. She needed the other evil or dark witches to work for her and they didn't seem to be doing that, except for Lorissa's daughter and since she was no longer gaining strength, she had to assume that was a failed attempt on her life. Other than Lorissa dying or her lifting the curse, there was no other alternative but to stay put in her box and try not to go crazy. She did keep her ears open to any sound and remained very alert while she waited for whatever it was that was coming. She had a feeling it wouldn't be too long of a wait either. She used to hear sounds from the creatures in the forest, but now it seemed everything they said was hushed as though they were keeping something from her with their whispers, or maybe they'd put more dirt on her box and it was muffling the sound. Either way she didn't like not being able to find out anything. Silence was very boring.

When breakfast was finished the coven began to discuss just exactly what they would be doing. They needed to make sure every single one of them was doing their part, standing in their spot and that nothing distracted them. This was a very important addition to Zythora's bounds and if they were not in sync, then they could end up freeing her. It shouldn't happen due to the wording of the curse, but stranger things had happened in the past. They tried to never leave anything to chance.

So the order of things was the coven would hold hands and stand in a circle around Cassandra. They would be facing her while chanting and focusing on the wand held high in her hand so all their power would go straight to it to be refocused by Cassandra and directed toward Zythora. They would be in alphabetical order, because order was imperative to a good spell. The circle would consist of Ariel, Evangeline, Laila, Melek, Miranda, Parisa and Seraphina in that order. Their chant was very familiar to them as they'd done the same thing when Lorissa bound and banished Zythora over six hundred and fifty years prior.

Powers that be, give us the power
Powers of light, expel the darkness
Powers that be, give us the power
Powers of light, expel the darkness.

Once Cassandra felt the power was strong enough, she would utter the spell to create the bubble, then she would fold it completely around Zythora's box.

They all knew their places and what to do.

They each chose their spot. Miranda didn't know for sure if Javan could be detected by Cassandra for her to wield the powers there, but if not, she still knew it was exactly dead center of Drenidore and that was where her concentration lay. Javan was still going to be there, several feet away in order to watch the bubble being formed to ensure it was sealed.

Sisters, are we ready?
Yes Miranda, they chanted as one voice.

Cassandra raised her wand high above her head and began the ceremony. "Continue to chant sisters, chant for the powers of goodness to overcome the powers of darkness while I speak the spell. So they began to chant louder:

Powers that be, give us the power
Powers of light, expel the darkness
Powers that be, give us the power
Powers of light, expel the darkness.

She joined them in her mind and very soon she began to see, actually see the box bound in chains buried inside the earth in the middle of the forest. Once it was all clear and she felt the power circling around her and the wand almost humming, it was so alive with power; she began her spell just as Lorissa had so long ago.

"I call upon the Gods and Goddesses to give me strength and power to overcome this wicked witch who has wrought so much evil upon this land. Give us the power to increase our safeguards around her until the time I can utter the spell to destroy her and end her curse. I command that Zythora be encased inside a magic bubble while bound in the box, buried in the center of Drenidore. I command this until we break the curses she has decreed on these two kingdoms! Do this for me. So Mote It Be. I command this spell to be in place for as long as I live upon this earth or until I release it because we've found a way to kill Zythora and release everyone from the curses she has uttered against the inhabitants of Drenidore and Airamoor."

Cassandra felt the power leave her wand and her body as she spoke the words of the spell. She knew the spell had worked and the coven stopped chanting and they all sat down on the ground to rest. It was a lot of power and energy that passed through them all that day and they would need to rest for the remainder of it. The older witches would probably need to rest a lot of tomorrow as well.

After about half an hour had passed, they began to get up and make their way to the house. They all went to bed and slept half the day and when they awoke, they were all famished and needed to replenish their physical strength.

With a small wave of her hand, Miranda had filled the table with meat, cheese, bread, broth, tea and fruits for them to eat. They would have a stronger meal that night which would finish what they needed to be refreshed. They all would have regained their powers by that time, except the oldest ones.

Cassandra was next to arrive after Miranda. Mama, it felt like a million bees buzzing in my head and zipping around throughout my body. I was so charged with energy, my skin felt like it was moving of its own accord. No wonder we were so weak after, we'd expended all we had. I understand now how you all defeated her way back then. She must have been overly exhausted as she only had her energy to spend and she must have truly spent it all. I picture her like a rag doll when she had finished. I had the energy of eight coursing through me and I still felt like I'd run all day without a rest. It was amazing though, I must say. If it's ok with you, I'll grab a plate and head to the forest. I'm sure Javan will be there to fill me in about the bubble and to inquire of our well-being. I won't be too long.

Very well dear. I'll call the others while you

make yourself a plate. Be sure to take a cup of juice with you, you'll be thirsty. Eat slowly, but eat it all. Your body needs to rejuvenate itself.

True to his word, Javan was there and had been since he'd made his way back there after the ceremony. It was a thing to watch Cassandra, I wish you could have seen it. The glass came from nowhere. It bended and folded digging down beneath the box she was in to totally enclose it under the ground. I only knew because of the dirt flying around due to the box being partially uncovered as each section was completed. It was very tricky how you kept her buried while you worked the additional layer of protection around her. Keeping it buried kept your magic from being absorbed from the curse. There wasn't enough exposed at any given time for it to be destroyed. I don't think we'll have to worry about her any more until you're ready to take her out.

Thanks so much for being there to see it work. It relieves me to know for sure it did. That was a BIG spell with a lot of power behind it. It would have been awful had I messed it up!

We're all eating and then going to rest till dinner and then off to bed. We should be totally recuperated by morning. I'll come down right after breakfast. If you're able to come, we'll talk a while then. Maybe I'll make my dragon. I think I'll make him small enough to hold in my hands and then as he learns I'm his master, I'll start to grow him a little at a time, and help him learn his powers and magic. He needs to know what he can do besides scare people. I may have to do some more research myself on that. I know what to feed him and how to care for him, but that's all I really know. Maybe you could ask Angelica if she has any knowledge of dragons that would help me.

I'll be here Cassandra. Have a wonderful evening and I'll be sure to ask her about dragons. If she knows, she'll tell me. Good night.

Good night Javan! She smiled, waved and turned to head across the field to her bed.

16 – Magic and a Dragon

Cassandra could barely wait to get to the forest the next morning when breakfast was over. Her body was charged with energy. Not like yesterday, but because she was so excited to make her dragon.

Wait just a minute, young lady, you have chores to be done first.

Oh, I forgot mama. With that Cassandra waved her hand, it was barely noticeable but the entire house was clean. Not just the kitchen, but the entire house. There was not a single bit of dust, dirty clothes or dishes. Nothing was out of place. Clothes were mended and windows were shined. The pantry was well stocked, the scratch in the table was gone and the silver had been polished. In less than 30 seconds from the time she waved her hand, she was out the door with a shout that chores were done.

Miranda looked around the room and just shook her head. She could only imagine what powers Cassandra would have now had she been taught magic when she was taught to walk and talk. This might take a little adjusting to for both of them since Cassandra was barely giving a thought to what she was performing with her magic.

She could already see Javan waiting at the edge of the forest and she waved to him as she ran across the field toward where he waited.

She plopped down in the grass and asked was he ready.

I think so. I've never seen a dragon before. Queen Angelica said to tell you she knew very little of them first hand; but she did know quite a few things that was told to her by a very reliable source. She said that you would be the only one to command him and he would be very loyal and do exactly what you told him. That's how they were and the bond was even stronger when you are the one who creates them. She also said it was smart to start with him being little till he gets used to you. She said to be sure and pet him a lot. It gives you the personal connection and they learn your scent. They especially like their chins to be scratched; gently, but scratched. Look him in the eye when you talk to him and you'll always have his attention. He will want to please you because you have created him.

You need to be the only one to feed him, at least for the first year. He needs to know he can depend on you. Let him kill his own food. Even when he's little, make him a tiny mouse and let him catch, kill and eat it. It's something about self-esteem; I think was the word she used.

He needs to know he's valuable. Tell him how much you love him and how he is the best thing you've ever had. Tell him he is your friend. Hold him to your heart and let him feel the beat of it. He'll know his life depends on your life and because of that he will be your protector. You need to praise him for things he does and he needs your approval and needs to know you are proud of him. He will want to make you happy.

It is of the utmost importance that as you build this relationship that you love, need and trust him to be your friend and ally; and make sure he knows he can depend on you to take care of him and be his friend and ally.

You must also make sure he knows you are the boss. He needs to know he will be punished if he doesn't do the things you ask of him. Stress the fact that he has a responsibility and he wouldn't want you to be disappointed in him. He must always respect you as he would his mother because you in reality are. He needs to understand his magic will come from you and without you his magic will fade until it's gone.

He has to understand he will be kept a secret most of his life, but he has a great role to play in the near future and throughout your lives.

Because of the secret, you may be his only friend and definitely his only daily contact. If you find an animal he is especially fond of eating, you must save that for a special day or treat because he accomplished something wonderful or amazing. He should feel that you are the only one in the world who can give him this special treat; and without you, he may never have it again. Protecting you is his primary goal in life and it is an honor to be the one chosen to do it.

She said once you've instilled these beliefs in him, and it will take time for him to realize them all; then you will have the creature that you need and the assurance that you will be protected at all times.

She said this instinct of his to protect you is what will help you defeat Zythora. So nurture it as best you can because it truly will be what saves your life when you turn sixteen and speak the spell to destroy her.

Wow, Javan, that's a lot, but it seems like just what I would do for him anyway. I take care of the chickens and cattle already, like they're my friends so working with Greargon should be easy. But then again, I'll really be his mama, so it may not be as easy as I thought. I'm a pretty good girl, but sometimes my mama has to get after me to do something, or punish me when I

don't do my chores. OK, here goes.
She thought real hard about what she wanted
her dragon to look like and how big she
wanted him to be, then barely moved a finger
and he was sitting on her outstretched hand.
He was exactly as she'd described him to her
mother except he was only ten inches tall. She
looked him straight in the eyes, smiled and said
"Hello Greargon, I'm your mama." And she
stroked his head, all the way down his back to
the end of his tail, then reached up and
scratched his chin. He pushed his head into the
palm of her hand and rubbed gently as if he
was hugging her. He wrapped his tail up
around her wrist and gave a little roar.

You are the most beautiful dragon I've ever
seen! You are perfect. I can see someone
being afraid of you at first sight which is a very
good thing, but I also can see how once they
meet you, they'll love you as much as I do! I
am so thrilled. You look exactly as I imagined
and described you. I was not expecting you to
turn out so exact, so amazing, so wonderful! I
love you so much Greargon. She petted him
again and rubbed her cheek along his face,
showing him only love and no fear.

She smiled and turned him to face Javan and
introduced them. She explained Javan
couldn't leave the forest, and they could not
enter it yet. But he was their friend and he

would help them any way he could because that's what friends do. She petted him some more and told him how beautiful he was with his beautiful blue back and shimmering teal underwings. How majestic his crown of horns were about his head. She would smile and speak in a gentle voice, as she talked. After a little more petting, she produced a bowl with water for him to drink and a one inch long mouse, not counting the tail. She held it in her hand to make sure he saw what she did. She set Greargon on her knee and then moved her hand toward the ground, opening it ever so slightly so he could see the mouse. He leaned toward it and she closed her hand. He looked up at her and she said, you must wait till I say you can. Greargon looked a little sad but watched her again move her hand towards the ground. He waited patiently, looking back and forth from her hand to her face. When her hand was resting on the ground, she spoke.

"Now, go ahead." She said as she opened her hand to let the mouse run off her fingers. Greargon jumped off her knee and grabbed the mouse before it hardly realized it was free. He gulped it down very quickly and then sort of smiled. Then he stretched his wings and attempted to fly, but he didn't have enough strength as he was still a baby.

Cassandra quickly picked him up and held him

up to her cheek and told him she'd help him and that he had done good waiting until she said he could. She told him to let her know when he was hungry and she'd give him some food. If he didn't tell her before, she'd give him some about the same time every day. He sort of squeaked at her and rubbed her cheek with his head.

You'll be able to speak to me very soon, I'll be giving you some magic tomorrow and then I'll help you learn how to use it. I'll always take care of you, you are my little dragon and I love you very much. Your name means Champion of the Skies and I think it will suit you nicely once you get your magic, learn to fly, and grow into a proper size dragon. I'll be with you the whole way to help you learn what you need to do. I'll protect you and you'll protect me.

We will be best of friends and you will grow very big and tall. As big as that cottage over there. That is our home, so you will need to recognize it and take care of it as well.

Greargon just nodded at her, rubbed her cheek again and smiled. It was a little odd, his smile, but it was his smile and that's all that mattered. She scratched his chin again and then pulled him against her to cuddle some.

I'm going to take him to see mama, we'll be

back tomorrow for more training and conversation with you. Have a great rest of your day Javan.

Let's go Greargon, you have to meet my mama. She's wonderful. You will love her too and she will help me teach you things. I'm so excited I can hardly stand it. You are mine! All mine! And you are beautiful!

He's a very nice dragon Cassandra. I like his coloring and he seems to have a nice demeanor as well. If you always treat him like you are supposed to treat everyone, he'll stay that way and he'll love you unconditionally. I think you chose wisely. He suits you, much more than a cat would. I think a dragon is most appropriate for the witch that's going to destroy Zythora. Are you ready to practice your magic today?

I am mama. What will I be doing this time?

I believe you need to do your 20 minutes of conjuring stuff from nothing. Let's have you conjure water, fire, smoke and fog. These are all things you might use for camouflage. You don't want to flood anything or destroy anything with the fire, but you need to use them to become invisible to someone near you.

She immediately caused a thick fog to roll in, actually roll out of her, it seemed. It was all around them both and the air was filled with it. Miranda could not see her hand in front of her face. This is definitely a way to keep from being spotted, she told Cassandra.

As soon as the words were spoken, the fog was gone and was replaced by smoke. Not a choking kind of smoke, just hard to see through and around. I can see you Cassandra, but if you move around some, it would be hard to tell exactly where you were as you would be swirling the smoke around you as you moved.

Now try the water or fire and think about being totally invisible, like with the fog, but fitting into a natural setting where someone wouldn't suspect you to be hiding. They'd just think they were enjoying the nature around them, or watching the fire burn with no one attending it, as if they'd run away all of a sudden.

She thought for just a minute and created a beautiful waterfall between herself and her mother, with rocks around the sides and a nice pool at the bottom, flowing into a meandering stream that disappeared into the distance. Cassandra was quite proud of herself, but Miranda had to keep her in check. All she said was "Nice. I love waterfalls."

Another minute of thought and Cassandra smiled before disappearing into a roaring bonfire, taller than their cottage. The waterfall was totally replaced by the fire. Where the calm and serene had been a moment before, was now a raging fierce fire. It lapped flames of red, yellow, and orange high into the air. Miranda walked all around it and could not see Cassandra from any side.

This is very good, I've not been able to detect you at all. How have you hidden yourself in this fire?

Easy, I got in the middle. Cassandra said as she stepped out of the flames. She was not burned, had no smell of smoke on her, and no damage to her clothing. It was as though she'd never been in the fire. The fire was still raging and Cassandra smiled as she was sure this would impress her mother. She then produced sticks with chicken and vegetables on them, which she placed into the fire to roast them a snack.

Now, I'm impressed. Keep going. Show me what you've got.

Cassandra was elated that her mother was so impressed so she caused the fire to move into a large circle and placed chairs inside so they could enjoy the warmth against the chill in the air. Anyone outside the circle could only see a fire that appeared to be just a big bonfire, but inside, there was chairs, couches, a table full of food and drinks. I've put a door here mother in case we want to invite someone in that happens by. They can't see it, but a quick turn of the knob from inside and it swings open to let them in.

Ok, you're using your powers and doing what I've instructed, but you're also being creative with what you're doing. This has been an amazing show sweetheart! You truly are a gifted witch and are getting better every day.

I just want to make you proud mama. I really do.

I'm always proud of you dear. You are a good child. You listen to me and learn from what I tell you. You may not always understand why, but you rarely question me before you do something I've instructed you to do. Your questions come after your obedience and that always makes a mother proud. You remember the things I tell you are important and you treat others just like I've always told you. I think you'll see a lot more love and respect coming your way as you have contact with more and more people or other creatures you may encounter. Trust your instincts Cassandra, they're good. If you have a bad feeling about something or someone, it is probably very good to be extra cautious.

Make sure you instill all your good qualities in Greargon as well when you're teaching him. You've made him beautiful outside, now you have to teach him how to be beautiful inside so he can complement your love, interests and attitudes. He'll learn to mirror you so he can be an amazing force to be reckoned with whether he is using his charm or using his talons, teeth and fire breath to destroy someone. He'll have what it takes, just like you do.

OK, now for your twenty minutes in your other disciplines; and that should bring us close to dinner time. But before you start that practice session, do you think you could make a cloak of invisibility?

A what?

A barrier between us that allows me to see what's behind you, but not see you. You are standing beside me and wrap this cloak around you and you disappear. It doesn't have to be an actual cloak, but something you envision that you're placing around yourself to keep people from seeing you. You can then go wherever you want to go and see what you want to see without being detected by anyone present. Once you do it, I want you to move around some so I can see if I can detect any trace of your magic. If your cloak is strong enough, and I believe yours will be, then you not only will be invisible but your magic will be as well. You never know when you'll need to spy on someone, a witch even, and not be found out. Just don't you be using it on me, young lady. They both laughed.

Ok, I think I have it figured out, so here goes mama.

Well part one worked, I cannot see you after you placed the cloak. Talk and let me see if you can be heard.

Hello mama, I'm right here beside you.

If you said anything I couldn't hear you. Now you make it so I can hear you.

Cassandra thought really hard about what she wanted to happen, and then spoke. I'm here with you, Miranda, back from the grave.

That was great! I'm sure you could scare someone with that.

Now, move and I'll see if I can find you because as long as you're standing still, I can't detect where you are.

You're doing perfectly. If you were moving, I could not detect a thing. This is going to be amazing should you need it at any time, and you may. I'm not sure what arsenal will be needed to defeat Zythora.

That was pretty cool mama. I had fun running around you. I'll keep that in mind. It's just like the bubble really, only it's made just for one, and it moves with you. The bubble was fixed and we had to stay where it was.

You are correct and you're doing great with your studies. I'll be back in twenty for dinner. Cassandra practiced making things appear and disappear. Greargon watched her intently. He seemed to be absorbing everything she was doing. She made some treats for him and gave him a mouse to chase. He must have been hungry even after the snacks, because he grabbed the mouse and ate it in two bites.

What am I going to do with you? You're going to grow very fast at this rate. He smiled and hopped up on her knee. I think you want to grow up fast. He rubbed his head against her arm and she petted him and then scratched his chin. I'll give you magic tomorrow and we'll have some real fun. Maybe enough so you can fly.

She heard Miranda approaching from the house and realized she hadn't produced any dinner, so quick as a wink, she had a feast fit for a king all spread on a gorgeous mahogany table, with some expensive china laid out. She even had a water dish and a few more bites of meat on a plate for Greargon.

This is beautiful Cassandra and smells delicious too! They enjoyed their dinner and were only interrupted once when Greargon tripped over a fork when he was trying to make his way closer to Cassandra. She helped him up and all was well.

After dinner, she cleared the table, cleaned the house and went to her room to decide where Greargon was going to sleep and what kind of bed he would like.

He seemed to like her room. She made a basket first with a pillow inside. He laid on it, but then hopped back to her knee. She made a small bed that matched hers. He checked it out, but then hopped back on her knee. Then she created a cave with some hay inside. He went inside and stayed a few minutes, but then came back to rest on her knee. She finally got the message that while he may choose a bed later, right now he wanted to be next to her. She kept the two beds and gave them each a special place in her room, but then climbed onto her own bed with Greargon in her arms. She laid her head down on her pillow and he curled up against her stomach and fell asleep. She smiled because she remembered times she just wanted to be with her mama and would crawl into her bed and do the same thing.

She stroked his back and tail and whispered softly, it's ok mama's got you. It wasn't too long before he fell asleep as well with a smile on his face. She was very happy with her familiar. She had a dragon! Life didn't get much better than this.

Morning came way too soon, but Cassandra was well rested and was pleasantly surprised that Greargon had awakened her before her mother had called. He was hungry. She picked him up and headed to the kitchen. After fixing him a dish of water, she promptly created a mouse. He knew the second it appeared in her had. He was almost dancing with anticipation at the tasty feast coming his way. She made him sit and wait until she gave the command. This time she let the mouse get three feet away before she told him to go ahead. He had sat very still, waiting, watching her then the mouse and back to her again; anticipating the moment he could spring into action and enjoy his meal. He was very fast once she gave the command to go. As soon as he'd finished eating it, she scooped him up and praised him for waiting for her command. She petted him and scratched his chin and held him close, telling him how much she loved him and how proud of him she was.

It was then her mother came in. Cassandra looked up and said I've got this and immediately the table was full of delectable breakfast goodies. French toast seemed to be the item of choice with fresh fruit, a drizzle of chocolate and a dusting of powdered sugar.

Ummm, Cassandra you are a very good chef! She managed to thank her between bites as she was hungry and eating a little fast this morning. She gave Greargon a couple berries and he liked them very much.

Mama, will you supervise me giving him some magic this morning? I don't want anything to go wrong.

Tell me what you want him to be able to do with this magic and we'll decide if it's the right amount.

Well I want him to be able to fly and talk to me.

Is that all?

I think so. Is there something else I should consider?

No dear, I was just surprised you didn't want him to do more. It's good you're going slow. Give him time to learn how to fly before he grows too much. He'll see how it all works and have an understanding of speed and such before he's huge and has a lot of body to launch, land and control during flight. You have a very good head on your shoulders my dear.

Thanks mama, you taught me everything I know. Again they both laughed, but Miranda knew her daughter had meant every word in the best possible way there could be.
Now he just needs a sprinkle. Concentrate on the skills you said you wanted him to do. You want him to learn to fly with precision. Speed will come later, so keep that in mind when you bestow your magic on him.

Cassandra took a deep breath closed her eyes and saw herself talking to Greargon and watching him fly. He wasn't going fast, just making incredible maneuvers. Then she spoke the words. **Powers that be, extend powers to me. Powers to endow my dragon with what he needs to speak to me and fly accurately. Do this for me. So mote it be.**

When she opened her eyes, Greargon looked up at her and said Thank you mama, I love you so much!

Oh Greargon, you can talk to me! Now let's see you fly. Look at where you want to go and then flap your wings and you will lift from the ground. The harder you flap, the faster you will go, but you need to practice steering with your head and your tail. Your head is for main direction and your tail is for turns. Give it a try.

He looked rather skeptical, but trusted her with all his being. He looked up at her as she stood over him, and began flapping his wings. When he lifted from the ground, he quickly looked down and he faltered a little.

Keep your eyes on where you want to be. Now keep flapping your wings and fly up here in front of me.

He did just that and she caught him and let him rest on her arm.

That was SO cool! I want to fly more!

Ok, if you're rested enough, take off. Show me what you've got, but remember to make turns you have to use your tail. Go slowly and try different things. It won't take you long to get the hang of it all and you'll be flying circles around me.

He did just that. He only had a couple bobbles. Cassandra even caught him once before he hit the ground. He'd swung his tail too fast and it turned him further than he wanted to go and he lost his balance. That was scary, but I know I can do this.

You're right my funny little dragon, you can do this! Just keep flying. I'll run with you through the field to the edge of the forest where Javan can watch. Whatever you do, do NOT go into the forest, it will drain all your magic and you will be trapped there. Make sure you're in control before you get within 20 feet of Drenidore. I don't want to lose you! I love you so much I couldn't bare it.

I'll watch, now let's go. With that he took off flying and Cassandra took off running alongside him. Miranda watched from the house and was so proud of them both. She saw them collapse near the forest and start talking to Javan. Greargon was flying close to her, but catching a lot of bugs and eating them. Then he spied a field mouse and took off after it, he was headed straight for Drenidore. Cassandra noticed him at just the last second to be able to stop him. She screamed for him to stop and shot a glass wall up in between him and the edge of the forest. He heard her and started to slow, but was too close to the glass and he slammed into it not so easily. She knew he'd be sore and bruised, but he was safe and that's what mattered.

Greargon, you can't get distracted when you're close to something as dangerous as Drenidore. Remember I told you it would suck all your magic away and you'd be trapped. You had been snacking on bugs, so I know you were not starving. You could have ruined your life for the next three years all because of chasing a mouse for your lunch. There are many dangers in this world that you'll have to be careful of. I'm not mad at you, I'm just sorry you had to get hurt to be stopped. I love you too much to lose you. Promise me you'll pay more attention or we won't be able to play so closely or visit our friend Javan as often.

I'm sorry, I promise not to be distracted and will work on perfecting my focus. Thanks for saving me. I love my magic and want to keep it forever. I want to keep you forever too. I want us to always be together. Would you please give me some food to eat. I really am very hungry as I've used up all I have flying.

Of course. Here's a ground mole for you. You need to try new flavors and see what you like best.

I sure liked that mole. He was tasty.

We'll start to vary your diet more so you'll get all the vitamins and minerals you need to keep you strong and active. Just remember, any time you want something, just ask. Oh, and I was very impressed with your flying skills.

Really? I'm so glad! It's exciting to fly. When I get big, I'll take you flying with me. You will love riding on my back! I'll be careful and take care of you, like you take care of me. I love you.

Oh Greargon, we're going to make a great team and will always be friends! Javan I'm hungry would you like some lunch too?

I'd love some chicken, but please don't cook mine. In my wolf form, I like it freshly killed best of all, but if you don't want to see all that, I'll take it ready to cook without all the "Trimmings" if you know what I mean.

Yeah, I know, blood and guts! She laughed.

At least you didn't get all queasy when you said it. There might just be hope for you yet. I wasn't so sure since you're a girl.

Keep that up and I won't feed you lunch at all.

Before he could say a word, she tossed a chicken into the forest and he caught it in his strong jaws and began to eat his lunch. She produced another mole for Greargon and whisked her mother from the house to the edge of the forest with her. By the time her mother got there in like 3 seconds, she landed on a lovely blanket and there was food all around, fruit, sandwiches, punch and little cakes for dessert.

Sorry if I startled you mama, but everyone was hungry so I hurried. You ok?

Of course dear, I'm actually used to being transported places. Usually I'm the one doing it, but it feels the same. Just a little more of a surprise when it happens by someone else and I'm not expecting it. This looks great by the way. I think you shall start transporting yourself places. We'll do that right after we enjoy our magnificent lunch you've made us. I don't think you'll really have to have training as perfectly as you moved me, but you can practice some. Now let's eat, I'm hungry too.

Greargon flew around them a few hundred times as they ate.   He would dip low and get a grape, then soar high above their heads and dive back down.

Miranda smiled at Cassandra and then looked up and spoke to Greargon. You're really getting the hang of it now. Hopefully no more slamming into protective walls. He looked a little sheepish and said he'd learned his lesson.

You two come in shortly. We'll start practicing

your new ability tomorrow instead, I have a few things to do. You need to rest tonight. Good night Javan.

Good night Miss Miranda. I'll see you tomorrow.

17 – Training and Moving On

Greargon and Cassandra were up right on time and ready to start their day. They were excited about her new project. They had breakfast, she did her chores, and hurried outside to await her mother for training. While they were waiting, she worked with Greargon on his flying skills. She'd hold up something for him to land on, or make a circle with her arms and he'd have to fly through it. She sat on the ground and he would fly under her knees as if it were a bridge he was flying under. He could do all that now, while he was so small, but there would come a day that the only part of him that would fit under her would be his back when all of her body were sitting there riding through the skies on the best thrill ride in the world. They had been playing or training actually for about an hour when Miranda joined them.

Ok mama, we're ready. What do I do first?

Well, I think we'll do weight and distance trials to see how strong you are. I want you to create a fifty pound boulder and toss it in the air fifty times, then across the field fifty times. We'll check to see if you're making it the whole way or if you're getting weaker the longer you toss it. Then you'll do a one hundred pound one the same way.

Ok, it's been half an hour and I've completed all those things, now what?

You will make yourself disappear and reappear a hundred feet away, then five hundred, then a thousand feet. Once you've done that and returned each time, then you'll take me with you on each trip. After that we'll see if you can transport us a mile. If you can do that we'll see if you can take us all the way to Lorissa's castle in one leap

Why can't I just start with a mile?

If you were going to build muscles, would you start lifting fifty pound weights? No, you would start with one pound weights and you would work up to the higher weights. You have to build your muscles, whether they are physical muscles, mental muscles or magic muscles. You have to start small and perfect your craft.

Ok, I understand.

Within another half hour, they were sitting having tea with Lorissa. She could not believe how quickly Cassandra's powers were developing and still getting stronger. She really didn't have a lot left to learn until her dragon was fully grown and ready to be trained to help her.

We'll just live as normally as we can for the next two years then we'll start Greargon's training. He's a really fast learner and I don't expect him to take very long in his training either. It could be the magic he received from Cassandra that makes him a fast learner. Her magic is so strong and he got a dose of hers, so I'd expect him to learn quickly and grow strong much faster than normal. We'll live here as planned, but will pop back to our house to visit Javan and Angelica to keep them informed of anything going on and especially when the day approaches, they'll need to know the plan.

Miranda, this is wonderful, hopefully we'll be able to all live free again in love and happiness. This land has been bleak for too many years

I know and I believe more and more every day that Cassandra and Greargon can do this for everyone.

The day she does, she will be crowned the new Queen of the White Witches.

Lorissa?

No, I did my part in saving the kingdom and making a way of escape. She'll be the one to finish the work, she deserves it more than anyone. It won't matter that she will only be sixteen years old, she will be strong enough to rule with no one trying to push her aside. You'll be by her side for many years, advising and guiding her and she'll have Greargon to protect her. They look like they're already inseparable. She loves my castle and has improved it tremendously with her tender loving care. She deserves this Miranda and don't you try to persuade her otherwise, you know it's true.

I do, but I love you so much, it will be hard for me to see you step down.

I'll still be around you know, I just won't be in charge any longer. I'm not planning on leaving any time soon. I think our new queen may even grant me the privilege of living out my days here with her and her family.

We'll be back in a fortnight to take up residence again. She'll want to go back to school and I'm sure she'll be having Peter and Millie come to visit and get acquainted with her dragon.

Those two weeks passed more quickly than most. It was time to leave and it was very hard for Cassandra to tell Javan good-bye.

I know you'll be back, but I'll miss seeing you every day.

We'll miss you too, but we have to be there for final training and for me to attend school. I'll transport us back every few days for a short visit and when Greargon grows enough to carry me, we'll fly back to see you. I won't forget you my friend. We just have to wait for the time to be right and then we can be together all we want. If you still want to see me then. Time changes things and it may change how you feel for me.

It won't.

Don't look so glum. I can't stand the thought of you being miserable the whole time I'm gone. I care about you and so does mama and Greargon. You'll have Angelica and surely you have some family around and a few friends.

I do, they're just mostly so depressed about losing their magic and love, not being able to leave the forest and the fact that everyone they see feels the same way. They've just lost hope. If they could only see you and know what you can do, they would once again have hope; but they can't and they don't, so depression is a major issue inside Drenidore. I can only imagine the same is true in Airamoor. I understand you have to go, I'll just miss you. Do what you need to do and come visit as often as you can. I'll be thankful for every minute I can get and the time together will be much sweeter since you'll be missed so.

I agree. It will be hard not to see your face each day after breakfast, but we have to do this to fix the wrongs of the past. Until we see each other in a few days. He couldn't say it, he could only nod and turn slowly away.

She did visit him two to three times every week and she continued her training of Greargon. He had grown twelve feet in the year that had passed. He was probably a little more than a third of his final height. He should be at his full grown height somewhere around 36 feet, give or take a foot or two, by her 15th birthday. He would also be breathing fire by then, or around that time anyway. That would be another challenge helping him learn to control that.

She, Peter, and Millie had worked and played with him. They were nearly as close to him as she was. He was loyal though and didn't give them quite the love, respect and attention he gave her.

She had made full confession to them both that she was a witch and what her destiny was. She explained for them to be able to have fun with her and Greargon, they had to know. It's not easy hiding a dragon, especially when you don't want to and he doesn't want to be hidden. They kept him from the town folk so he was their own adventure and they were having the time of their lives.

Cassandra was feeding him calves, sheep, or hogs most of the time, but he liked donkeys too. For a snack, he'd have a turkey or a few chickens. She loved talking to him. Even being a witch and knowing all about magic and how nothing was impossible, it still seemed incredible that he could talk. He had lots of questions, but she supposed she did too growing up and still had them and they probably would the rest of their lives. She also liked playing games, but flying was her favorite thing to do with him. He was big enough to carry her short distances; but he was gaining strength every day. They were a happy foursome and spent most of their spare time together. Sometimes Cassandra would help them finish their chores so they could all be together for training and play. They would hide and Greargon would have to sniff them out.

Cassandra had made his cave as he was too big to sleep in her room all the time, but sometimes she'd use magic to shrink him down half his size so he could cuddle up in her bed. Other times, she'd take a blanket and snuggle up next to his side on his tail. He had even sneaked into her room quite a few times, crawling on his belly to fit through the doors. The palace had high ceilings, but the doors were only eight feet tall. They didn't care if they were cramped, cold or hot as long as they were together.

She transported them to see Javan some days and sometimes they flew together to visit. He did mope a lot during the school day, while the children were having lessons, but he would fly and use his time to build his strength. He wanted to be the best dragon ever and he didn't mind working at it either. He was just lonely without the children around to play with.

Cassandra knew this and asked her mother if she knew what to do for him. Should she make another dragon to keep him company?

NO! You can't do that. Dragons are loners when it comes to other dragons. They all want to be superior to all other dragons so they don't get along very well. They will come together to mate, but then the mother is left to raise the baby once it hatches. I don't think another animal would serve the purpose either as he would likely eat it one day when he was especially hungry and not yet meal time. I'll make time to visit and read to him an hour each day. I'll read him some stories about other dragons so he can see how they acted and lived.

I think he'd like that mama and that will give him something else to look forward to while I'm at school.

Why don't you tell him and I'll decide which stories I'll read or tell him.

She started reading to him the very next day and after each story, he would ask dozens of questions and not just about the dragon, but its owner or companion. He asked about the powers and how they could be better developed; and what happened to them when they were left alone like if their owner was killed. He wanted to know what his existence would be after Cassandra if he survived her. He wanted to know how to find a mate and if he did and they had a dragon, would he ever see it or want to. He wanted to know about the feelings dragons had. There was a lot to tell, and just like humans there were a lot of different feelings. There was no right or wrong way to feel about a situation or how to handle a tragedy, all dragons were different, depending whether the dragon had a good heart or an evil one.

He worried about Cassandra and Miranda was glad of that because it meant he still put her first and that was vital to their plans. Time was flying by as the two grew older, stronger and wiser, but yet it seemed to drag by for all of them. They wanted the curse lifted, but they had to wait. They thought they were strong enough, but they had to wait. It was disheartening to sit around doing the same stuff every day and not be able to do what you wanted to because everyone was trapped in one way or another.

One day after their story and question session was over, Miranda decided it was time for her to have a question and answer session with Greargon. Have you noticed any changes in yourself. Like a burning in your throat or a burp that seems to raise food back up from your stomach?

Yes, occasionally I have done that. Does it mean something?

Maybe, have you had any dreams?

Only one. I dream that every meal I eat is on fire. The cow is fine when Cassandra makes it for me, but when I open my mouth to eat it, it's suddenly in flames. I've had that one a lot lately.

Good, I think it's nearing the time you will be able to breathe fire. I want to tell you a little about it so you'll be ready when it happens.

I'd appreciate that. Cassandra hasn't mentioned it to me yet.

She doesn't know what to tell you so she didn't know how to approach you about it. You will begin to feel a burning in your throat, almost like you ate something hot. Since you've never eaten anything cooked, you won't know right away what it is, but it will feel different. You may notice some spots on your body that seem lighter and you may burp more after eating as your body will be struggling to function in a different way. You may even be thirsty more often. When these things start to happen, first of all we want to keep you near water. We may have to put a stream through your cave and a pond near the castle. If you should breathe fire, we'll need to be able to put it out quickly and you drinking something will help a lot.

When Cassandra made you, she gave you some beautiful designs that will appear as the fire builds within you, just before you let it out. That's why I mentioned the spots. The designs will glow from the fire within and you will be even more magnificent than you already are. It will, however, give your enemies or opponents a heads up that you are about to send fire their way and they will scatter; which could cause you to miss your target.

It doesn't really come from your stomach or lungs. You have a gland in your throat that is filled with very flammable oil, if you will. When you become angry your blood boils and it ignites this oil. When you draw in a deep breath, the burning oil is gathered with the air and when you expel the excess air not required for breathing, it contains the fire and whatever direction you send the air, you'll actually be sending the fire. If I pick up a handful of sand and blow on it. It will fly off my hand and scatter. That's how simply you direct the fire. Once you start expelling the fire, it will continue coming for as long as you blow the air out. Once you've exhausted that supply you'll have to take another deep breath and do it again. You will need to be careful between blasts of fire when you're taking that next breath, as you will be vulnerable then and subject to attack.

Once you actually begin to see the fire when you cough or burp, we'll have to begin immediate training. We'll have to have several practice sessions in order to help you gain control and precision. You will need to learn to control your fire and your breathing. If we need the fire lit in the house, we don't want you burning down the entire house. Likewise, if you are trying to destroy someone or something, you don't want to waste any of your fire by blowing in the wrong direction. You'll need to focus and not be swayed by your anger.

Dragons are the only creatures on earth that can breathe fire, and with that comes great responsibility. If you or those you love are in danger, certainly use your gift. Do not let it go to your head. It is not something to do to impress someone or prove you have something they don't. You need to protect your gift and cherish it as you are a rare and special creature.

I understand. I'll let you know the minute I start showing any symptoms of fire breathing. If I start to get out of control, I'll drink and I'll try very hard not to let my emotions get the best of me. I know staying calm is key for the guaranteed success of mastering the fire.

You are getting so big, more handsome and rather regal in appearance; especially if you pose with your shoulders back and head held high. Nearly another year has passed and we're nearing the final one before our quest is at hand. It seems so far away, but will be here before we know it, so the more we learn and practice, the better off we will be.

We'll be having a meeting of the coven next full moon and that is when we will devise our plan of attack to be executed on Cassandra's 16th birthday. You can let her know when you talk today after school. It will prevent us telling it over and over because Peter and Millie will be just as informed. You all can decide if you currently have any questions and start forming your own ideas of what will transpire that day; then everyone will bring their ideas together at the meeting. You two might want to ask Javan and Angelica to think of anything they may know or question as well. I know for a fact that we'll want everyone in Drenidore huddled in the four corners of the kingdom, so they'll be as far from Zythora as possible when everything begins.

I'll talk to the children, Miranda, and we'll go to Drenidore this weekend. We can spend most of the day there Saturday. Maybe we'll show off our skills too. I miss them and I know Cassandra does too.

18 – Early Plans

Mama! Mama! Cassandra screamed as she busted through the door and ran through the palace.

What is it child? I'm right here.

There you are! Mama, Greargon told me about your conversation. There's going to be a meeting and we're going to start making the plan of attack. Is it true?

Yes dear. We can't wait until the last minute. There may be some things that have to be set up or practiced. One thing I know for sure I want in place is an invisible dragon.

Invisible?

Yes. You need to work with Greargon and teach him how to become invisible. He can use the magic you gave him and if it's not enough, you'll need to give him a little more. I think it will be enough though, as he's grown stronger, so check before you add to his powers. It's much harder to attack a dragon if you don't see him before he engulfs you in flames or swallows you whole. I'm sure he will be very instrumental in this battle. He'll need to practice a lot so there is no fading in and out. He'll need to be very quiet as he might be heard. Witches are very in tune with magic and we can sense it even though we can't see any effects of it yet. He'll need to practice his breathing as it requires a deep breath to fill his lungs to expel the fire and a breath taken in too quickly makes a noise. We have to be precise and perfect for this to work.

I want you both to practice more than ever so you are at the top of your game when your next birthday arrives. I'll be doing some practicing myself. We can't be caught off guard.

This birthday, however, I think we should do another giant cake and feast for the entire village. We'll announce ahead of time and get everyone to close their shops and come for dinner and prizes. We'll have games for the children and adults. It will be fun don't you think?

That will be great mama! Thank you so much. I love the idea. I appreciate this special birthday since I know my next one is going to be very trying. If we're successful though it will be the best birthday ever!

It's only a week away, so start making some invitations and thinking of games to play. Remember to put on the invitations that games will be played so they'll not wear their best clothes. Let's have some fun for a change and not be so serious. We'll have enough serious in the next year to last us a long time. Ask the children and your teacher, what games they'd like to play. Maybe we can have tournaments with prizes to be won. I also want to give something to every person that comes, so think about that. It can be a mere trinket to remind them of the good time they had at your party, or it could be something they could actually use on a daily basis or on special occasions. Maybe even something to trade for something they need. Think about it and we'll talk later.

Mama, can we introduce Greargon to the town folk? I think they would accept him, especially if we have him participate in some sort of event where they can get up close and personal with him.

I think you're right about the town folk. Talk to him and see if he's agreeable and see if he has any ideas of what game or event he could participate in.

I already know what event I want him to do if he's agreeable. I want him to give dragon flights.

I'm not sure the people will go for that. Would you let your child fly high in the sky with a dragon you'd just met?

Well, if we did it first and then I'm sure Peter and Millie would do it to show everyone it's safe. We can make a harness and saddle for two so they would be able to sit comfortably and have something to hold on. I will accompany everyone who wants to go, so they're not alone. Once everyone has had a ride, I'll take him for an exhibition ride and he can really let loose and do some tricks and stuff. Everyone would be amazed at his skills. It would be so much fun. Please can we give it a try?

We can, but don't be surprised if they're very cautious.

I'm going to go ask him now, and then we'll be right back for dinner and we can make more plans.

Ok. Remember we're all going to Drenidore tomorrow. I hope you reminded Millie and Peter. We'll start them thinking and making plans as well for next year. I'm pretty excited to see Javan and Angelica again. You and Greargon have gone quite a bit, but it's been just over a year since I've been home.

I already did mama, they'll be here bright and early for breakfast and the trip. They'll be happy to see you too, they always ask about you.

She was back in a very short time and had Greargon in tow. He said he would love to do it mama! Am I doing dinner or are you?

I already did it, slow cooked pork, beans and cornbread. Oh and if you've not eaten Greargon, I have four goats prepared for you.

I've not eaten and I've only had goat once before, is it my birthday or something?

Close enough. I hope you enjoy.

Oh, I'll enjoy and I'll be back in two minutes to chat while you two eat.

He's gotten so big mama, it's nice we can eat outside so he can be with us. He loves you too, almost as much as he loves me. It's also nice not to watch him eat just before I'm eating. He doesn't make much of a mess as most animals since he swallows his meal whole, but occasionally there's a good bit of blood involved.

This is good mama, did you slow cook it?

If you mean the human way, yes I did. I like the smell it creates in the house. It adds to the experience of eating. Doesn't taste any different, but it builds anticipation all day long.

I've thought of a few events we can have at my birthday party.

Good. Fill me in.

For the adults, I think the men could have a shooting contest and the winner gets a gun for his prize. I also think they could have an arm wrestling contest with a gold coin as the prize. The women could have a pie baking contest with the prize being a new set of pans and they could also play a game where they have to use a broom to move a ball around from one end of a field to the other. They could play in teams and the women on the winning team would get new dresses.

I like those ideas, what do you have in mind for the children and the party favors.

Oh, the favors could be knives. Hunting knives for the men and kitchen knives for the women. The boys could get balls and marbles and the girls could get books and dolls. The babies could get a rocking horse to play with when they're a little older and a rattle for now.

I like those ideas too. Now what about the games for the children?

I'm not real sure about that. I was thinking maybe the boys could have a race to determine the fastest boy. We can play freeze tag with the boys and girls. The girls could have a jump rope contest, but I can't think of a second game for the boys or girls. Have you thought of any mama?

Why don't we have a fishing contest for the boys and a cake contest for the girls. But we still have to determine prizes for the children's games. Wait, I know what we can do. We can give fishing equipment, like line, a bucket, hooks and a net for the fishing champion and a gold coin for the winner of the race as well as the winner of the freeze tag game. The winner of the cake contest can get a set of pans, like the mothers, so they can practice cooking. And last but not least a gold coin for the jump rope contest.

They'll all get to take leftover cake and food home as we'll make three times as much as we'll need for people to eat at the party. It will be another good way to help them with a few more meals and tasty ones too. Special things they don't have often or may never have without us.

Mama, let's give a coin to every child who is brave enough to ride Greargon. That will be a good incentive to get them flying.

You're right and everyone will have a good

time. We can have musicians and dancing set up, maybe a dance contest for everyone, adults and children. Best dancers get new shoes and a new outfit of clothes.

If anyone says anything about any other games, even the day of the party, we can always come up with a prize right on the spot. We do have those skills.

You're funny mama. I know we can, we're witches and are very good at making things appear from thin air. We have the magic.

I think you two are incredible. One of you starts something and the other one has the ending. You work so well together. I'm always impressed with what you do and how you come up with all these fantastic ideas is beyond me.

Why thank you Greargon. That was a wonderful compliment. We do work well together, don't we Cassandra?

Yes we do mama. I'm getting really excited. I can't wait to tell everyone. I'm going to work on the invitations as soon as I finish my dinner and find the dessert you've made. There is one somewhere hidden, right?

Yes, child, I know you have a sweet tooth. I

made nut butter candy.

My FAVORITE! Thanks mama. I'm off to make the invitations. I'll get my art supplies and be right back Greargon, you can help me.

I'd be delighted.

Cassandra was very thoughtful about her invitations and Greargon was helpful in reminding her of all they'd talked about. When she then finally got it all in order like she wanted. She made the first poster and took it to show her mother. It looked like this:

HEAR YE! HEAR YE!

EVERYONE'S CORDIALLY INVITED TO THE PALACE TO ATTEND THE FIFTEENTH BIRTHDAY PARTY OF MISS CASSANDRA

**REGISTRATION BEGINS AT 9
GAMES START AT TEN SHARP, EVERYDAY ATTIRE**

**MEN: SHOOTING CONTEST   PRIZE: GUN
ARM WRESTLING CONTEST PRIZE: GOLD COIN**

**WOMEN: PIE BAKING CONTEST PRIZE: NEW PANS
TEAM BROOM BALL: PRIZE: NEW DRESSES**

BOYS: FOOT RACE   PRIZE: GOLD COIN

FISHING CONTEST PRIZE: FISHING EQUIPMENT

GIRLS: CAKE CONTEST   PRIZE: NEW PANS
JUMP ROPE CONTEST   PRIZE: GOLD COIN
BOYS & GIRLS WILL PLAY FREEZE TAG FOR A
GOLD COIN

SPECIAL RIDING EVENT FOR EVERYONE, GOLD
COIN FOR EVERY PARTICIPANT

PARTY FAVORS FOR EVERYONE!

This is great! I think you covered everything and made everyone feel wanted and I'm sure they will be excited by the prizes. We're going to have a wonderful time! We'll post this one in the square and you'll need two more to place at the school and the church.

I'm excited mama. It's going to be so much fun!

It is. Now let's get ready for bed, we've got a big day tomorrow. We're flying off to see our friends.

They were awakened by the laughter of two children peeking in through the window. Millie and Peter were too excited to sleep any longer so they showed up extra early.

Go on around and come in the kitchen, we'll

be right there. She waved her hand a bit and she was dressed, the bed was made, and she was heading for Cassandra's room.
I'm up mama she said, then immediately came out her door, dressed and ready to go.

By the time they'd both reached the kitchen, breakfast was on the table for the four of them, and Greargon was eyeing the cow that had just appeared in his cave.

After breakfast, which they all ate rather quickly, they headed to the courtyard. Greargon had just arrived.

Cassandra, why don't you make that saddle we discussed. We'll try it out today.

Yes! I thought about it last night. She closed her eyes and imagined a gorgeous silver saddle that would seat three people and had belts to help them stay in their seats. There was a strap that went all the way under Greargon's belly and attached to the other side, just like a horse, only much bigger. There were reins attached to a bit in his mouth. As soon as she opened her eyes, it was real.

I'm not too comfortable and can't talk well with this thing in my mouth. Can we try something different?

Oh, I didn't think about that. Horses don't talk and need guided, you talk and you decide where you're going. You know how to execute the plan. Let me see. She placed a strap around his neck that the reins attached to. Is this better or too tight on your neck?

No, this is nice, not tight at all and as it's midway of my neck, it won't fall down because my neck just gets bigger as it goes down and it's low enough not to choke me. I love the silver too.

It matches your chest. I thought about gold to match your eyes, would you rather have that?

No, I like the silver.

Ok, then let's go. And with that the three of them held onto Greargon's neck and he lifted them over his back and they slid off his neck into the saddles. That was pretty smooth.

It looked very easy Cassandra, I think the town folk will be able to do that for their rides.

Now that the saddle is perfect, I'll make a matching double saddle; as I doubt I'll take more than one passenger at a time at the party. Almost as soon as she'd finished speaking there was a matching "double" saddle on a wooden dragon next to Miranda.

That's perfect Cassandra. I'll be transporting myself there, so you all be careful.

Ok, see you there. The children waved to her and Greargon took off with his load, heading for Drenidore.

Miranda arrived first and went on into the house to check on things. She'd been there about five minutes when she heard the sound of his wings and came out to make sure their landing was perfect; and it was. She knew it would be, but she was a mother and everyone knew mothers were very protective of their babies, no matter how old they were, or how powerful. They all headed to the forest and just as expected it was only a minute before Javan and Angelica arrived to greet them.

They chatted for a while about the new children, how big Greargon was becoming, how much Cassandra had changed, and basically if all was well and anything new. They told them of the party they were having and how the coven was going to meet.

If you have any suggestions about next year's activities, please let us know. We're going to throw out ideas and see what the plan will be, then we'll work on perfecting it as the year progresses. I know for a fact you need to get every inhabitant in Drenidore to the four corners of the forest so they will be as far from the center as possible. She will not be a happy witch when we release her. We're going to put a shield up where we can so she stays longer in Drenidore than she would like to. It will drain her energy more and more with every second she is in there because of the curse.

In order for her to leave Drenidore, she'll have to release the curse, but I'm sure with hundreds of years to think about it, she'll have perfected her plan as well and will probably have another curse in mind just waiting to speak it. We'll have to be quick to act if we have hope of destroying her. We'll be practicing our maneuvers, spells, the chanting to connect all our powers into one and anything else we can think of.

Do you think if we dug trenches and everyone lay in them and covered ourselves with dirt, leaving just enough space to breathe, that it might protect us more? It might confuse her if she didn't detect any presence. I know with her buried in Drenidore, she didn't lose all her powers, so I'm thinking that might be a plan for us. I don't think it would hurt and it may just be enough to save us. There are also a few caves that many could hide in, they go pretty deep in the mountain.

It's a good plan, Angelica, just make sure the evening before, everyone gets to their spots so no one will be left out once everything commences and no movement will be made that day until you find out if you're safe or not. I'm not sure how early we'll begin, but I'll let you know closer to time once we decide. I hate you'll miss the fireworks, but I want you to be safe and right now, you're not in the best position to maintain your safety without a plan in place.

We've got just over a year. So anything you think of during that time, just let us know as soon as possible. Cassandra and Greargon will be making regular trips like always.

I can see hope rising in your faces. Hope changes every situation. I believe and I know you believe too. This is the time and Cassandra is the one.

Please tell your people how much hope you have and if they want to see Cassandra and Greargon, have them come to the edge here with you, so they can talk to them and maybe gain some hope as well. It would be nice if they were enthusiastic as well.

19 – The Party

Saturday arrived and Cassandra and Miranda looked like a whirlwind with their arms waving around, making things disappear and other things appear. All the food, the cake, which was shaped like a sleeping dragon by the way, the prizes, favors, games, chairs, tables, chargers for the people to take food home and decorations. Miranda wanted this party to be the best just in case she never had another one and if they did survive next year, they wouldn't have time or energy for a party and the sixteenth one is so special. If their plan works, it will be the most special ever, but still no party or cake even.

It was going to be touchy to introduce the dragon to the town folks as dragons had the reputation of being pure evil. Of course many thought that about witches, but these folks had seen past that and didn't mind the witches here and actually seemed to appreciate what they all did for them. They were certainly in for some new experiences. For those who totally accepted him, well they would have a dragon for a friend for the rest of their lives.

When the last one arrived, they began the line for lunch. People were chatting, laughing and commenting on how wonderful the food looked and smelled. When it was time to bring out the dessert, Cassandra was the one who was driving the team of horses pulling the wagon with the giant cake on it.

Ladies and gentlemen, I'd like to introduce you to my dragon. Everyone looked up as she spoke and she announced dessert was served. People talked about how amazing it looked and what a wonderful job she'd done decorating it. Many exclaimed how lifelike it looked. Once about half of them had been served cake. She again climbed to the seat in the front of the wagon and got their attention.

"I'm glad you all are loving my dragon cake." Cheers went up from the crowd and she spread her arms wide and said. "I want to introduce you to the real dragon and my friend, Greargon". Greargon swooped from the air into the courtyard just behind the wagon, so they could see him, but still had space between them. This time gasps went up and some took a few steps back. "There is no need to fear. He is very kind and loving. I wanted you all to meet him so you wouldn't be afraid should you see him flying by. He is my protector as well as yours. He loves our town and is hoping many of you will love him back." She nodded toward him and he began to speak in a most formal voice.

"My friends and countrymen, I am so excited to

get to meet you all today. Peter and Millie are already good friends of mine and have flown with me many times. We've had a saddle made and I'll am offering rides to anyone who wants to fly with me. Cassandra, Millie and Peter are first to fly so you all can watch, and they are all happy to fly with any of you, so you know you are safe. As Cassandra said, I love this place and I hope to be a welcome addition to the community. We're going for a flight now while you all consider whether you're flying or not."

The three children ran over to climb on board for the first flight of the day.

The line starts here for dragon rides. Greargon and the children will be right back, so anyone wanting a ride, please line up here. The people were slow to move as they were all watching the children strap themselves into the seat and grasp the reins as they lifted high into the air.

Ms. Catherine and LaDonna were the first to start the line. "I can't wait to see our town from the sky. This is exciting! Ms. Catherine said as she walked toward the starting spot for a ride.

Several children got in line as well, once they'd seen Ms. Catherine there. Parents were looking concerned, but at that point hadn't told any of them to move from the line. Most everyone had sort of gone back to the festivities while keeping a wary eye on the sky. It was a couple more minutes before Greargon and the children landed ever so gently and dismounted.

Cassandra, please don't change saddles, we want to ride together.

OK, we'll just leave it on in case others want to as well. Maybe some would like to try out the double saddle on the wooden dragon if they're too afraid to take a ride.

"Ladies" Greargon said as he extended his neck for them to take hold so he could lift them up to the saddle. Once they were strapped in, he took off. When they returned five minutes later, both women were laughing. They had thoroughly enjoyed their ride and told him so as they slid down his side to the ground. "We'll be back in just a few minutes as it looks like the line is short." They did go straight to the line and began waiting their turn as they talked to the ones in line, loud enough for others to hear of course. They weren't lying, they did have a great ride and wanted everyone to accept him and enjoy themselves. "I'm going to ask him to do a loop this time." LaDonna said as she was nearing the front of the line.

By the time the ladies had mounted for their

second ride, the line had more than tripled. It looked like they were all accepting him and putting their fears behind them.

There was not a single person who didn't like the ride and by the end of the day, everyone had taken a ride.

They enjoyed their games and loved their prizes and favors. It was a great party for everyone and Cassandra was the happiest of all. She would no longer have to hide her magnificent dragon. She could fly any time of the day and enjoy a stroll through the meadow without worrying someone would see.

Oh mama! This is a great birthday party! I'm so glad we did it this way. It was really a party for everyone and next year it will be a bigger party for sure!

I'm glad you had fun dear. I think by the time everyone eats some more and fills the containers to take home, we won't be left with too much food or cake.

She was right, just over an hour later everyone was preparing to leave. They were filling the containers with all the wonderful food and cake that was left. Everything was wonderful Cassandra, and Greargon was a hit. I think everyone walked over and told him good-bye before they left.

I'm so happy mama. This has been a great day for me and especially for Greargon.

It's always good when people come together and can have fun and friendship without harm or ill feeling toward anyone.
They rose early the next morning and went to visit Javan and Angelica again. They told them what a wonderful time everyone had and Greargon told some of the loops he'd done with the more adventurous riders.

They were excited to hear it. "You shouldn't have any problems from the town folk at all, now that they've had a great time and are in the know about you Greargon. That will make a big difference when you all battle Zythora next year. Javan and I are glad it all worked out."

As soon as this curse is over with, I'd really like a ride too, if you wouldn't mind Greargon.

Of course not Javan, you are my friend and I'll be happy to show you the world from the air.

I also wanted you to know I'm going to visit Airamoor. Is there anything I need to know or any message you want sent to anyone when I go?

Tell him I'm awaiting the day we can be together again and our love is rekindled. I long to have that emotion restored to me and I am sure the rest of our kingdoms will be just as happy. Thank you Miranda for the kind gesture.

You are most welcome. See you soon.

20 – Airamoor

Cassandra, I'm off to Airamoor. You and Greargon will remain here. I cannot enter Airamoor without succumbing to the curse, but I hope to speak with Baltaazar; he inside the walls and me outside the walls. Zythora was not careful in her spell. The city outside the walls and a fair amount of land was considered the kingdom, but she didn't specifically indicate that. She used the term Airamoor and that title is specific to the castle and lands within the walls. Palaces or castles are named and the surrounding land to a set boundary is normally called by the same name. She said she was going to curse the land surrounding the kingdoms, but when she spoke her spell, she didn't use the same wording, so the Kingdom of Airamoor was not cursed; just Airamoor, thus making the curse only effective inside the walls.

This is why I keep saying we'll develop the spells you will use and you will practice them until there will be no mistake when you say them. Everything will be thoroughly inspected. We leave nothing to chance. We cannot afford to make the same mistake she did. She was hurt, angry and young. You are young, but you are disciplined and methodical. You won't make that mistake because you will not be speaking from the heat of the moment, you will have ingrained the spells in your heart and mind.

You will be ready because you will have planned. I love you. Don't do anything dangerous while I'm away. I'll be back in three days if all goes well.

I love you mama, you be careful too. Lorissa will make sure we are well.

They hugged and Miranda waved her arm and was gone. She was at Airamoor. There was an inn very close to the palace gates. She would stay there. First thing after securing her room, she headed toward the palace.

I have a letter for the king. He is not expecting me, but I wish to have audience if at all possible. I've given him all the information in this letter, if you would kindly see that it's delivered, I'd appreciate it so much. She said as she cautiously slid the letter half way through the bars in the gate. She was very careful not to let her fingers extend past the boundaries of the walls.

It was immediately taken to the king and he opened it without sitting as he was hopeful that it was a letter extending some help or a solution to their problem. Her letter read:

Your Royal Highness Lord Baltazaar; I am but a humble servant to this and many other kingdoms. I am of the White Witch Coven of

Queen Lorissa. My name is Miranda. I would like to speak with you, but I dare not enter Airamoor because of The Curse and I am very aware that you cannot pass beyond the walls for the very same reason. So if it pleases Your Highness, I would that I could speak with you through a gate or in a corner where we could meet and speak over the wall. If that is not acceptable, but you are willing to hear what I've come to tell you, then send me back a message stating so and I'll write it all down and send back to you.

Your humble servant, Miranda

Advisor! Come quickly! I need your counsel.

The king's advisor was there within the minute asking what was wrong and what he could do for his king.

I am afraid to meet this woman. Do we have a way to check her out, or do I take my chances. I trust no one since the curse, especially someone who admits to being a witch, even if she does say she's a good witch. What think ye?

Your highness, I understand your trepidation and reserve in this matter. I do believe had she wished you harm, she would have just done whatever it is she wanted to do without regard as obviously she has the power to perform whatever is her will. However, I believe you to be safe in meeting with her; after all it was the white witches who bound Zythora and have kept her at bay these long six hundred and fifty some years.

I don't think I can. I am afraid. I cannot feel love, but I can be suspicious and afraid. I cannot lose any more or my mind shall join in and be lost as well. I know you have advised me well all these years, but I am just too afraid. I cannot lose my kingdom.

I understand my lord, do you want me to meet her and see what she has to say?

No, read her letter and you can join me when I get her next one. I'm going to tell her that we must correspond versus a meeting. I hope she will understand and tell me what it is she has to say.

Write her a note and I'll take it to the gate to be dispatched myself.

Miranda was disappointed that she could not actually meet with the king, but maybe this would be better. He'd have her word written and would not have to trust his memory. If he started doubting, then he could re-read the letter. So she thought long and hard about her wording and when her thoughts were gathered, she began to write:

Your Royal Highness Lord Baltazaar; I beseech your indulgence at what this servant has to say.

I wanted to tell you first of all that Queen Angelica is well and misses you. She would extend her love, but that is forbidden because of the curse as well. She thinks of you often and cannot wait for the day when her feeling of love returns and you two can be reunited. She is anxious to hear from you as it's been so many years without a word. She understands you are cut off from most things and people outside your walls, but hearing your voice and seeing your face is all she dreams of.

My daughter, Cassandra, will be sixteen years of age next year and has the ability, powers, and desire to break this curse. We believe she is the chosen one and she will have our coven helping her as well as her familiar, the magnificent dragon, Greargon. It has to happen on her 16th birthday. We have no choice about that. We are making plans and developing spells to be spoken to break the curses and restore both your kingdoms to their original glory and beauty.

The outside world is anxiously awaiting the day when life becomes normal again, for everyone and many are coming together in order to help this plan come to fruition. I wanted to give you hope. Hope you've not had for over six hundred and fifty years. Hope that will restore your faith in love and will give you the life you dreamed of with Queen Angelica.

We've already been able to strengthen our hold on Zythora and are honing our skills and strengthening our powers so that we will have no errors or mishaps at the ceremony. I also wanted to alert you about Greargon so you would know he is a kind and generous dragon. Don't mistake that as weakness as his powers are quite amazing and he's growing every day, physically, spiritually, mentally, and magically. He will do you no harm and will be a protector of Airamoor, Drenidore, and all the lands around and between.

Cassandra will turn 16 on the 11th day of the month of July. I do not know exactly what time that day as we've not decided, but I want you to be ready to fight should we break the curses, and release Zythora, but are unable to contain or destroy her. I fear her vengeance will be stronger than ever should that happen, but we are more confident in our plans, my daughter's powers and everyone involved in the plan to destroy her.

Respectfully,
Your loyal subject
Miranda, of the White Witch Coven

Miranda took the letter to the gate and instructed the guard to take it to the king as he was expecting it and that she would wait by the gate should he need to see her or have any messages for her.

His advisor was in with Baltazaar when the letter arrived. He read it with him and they were both excited that there was a plan afoot. They recognized the dangers as well. He didn't care if the plan failed and they were destroyed, it would be better than having to live another day, much less a thousand more years, as they were living now. It was horrible being trapped, alone, but not alone. Knowing you loved someone but not being able to see them, talk to them, or feel that love again.

Advisor?

I have nothing to say Sire, you know we're all miserable and if the attempt succeeds, then we're all free and happy. Should it fail and we're destroyed instead of Zythora, then we are still free and happy in the afterlife. Our best bet is to pray and offer any assistance that could be offered from inside these walls or whatever assistance our gold could buy them.

Our gold?

I know it's your gold Sire, but you rule the

kingdom so it is considered the kingdom's gold. Wouldn't it be better to be poor, free and happy than to be rich and captive in this palace as we've been all these years?

You are correct. No wonder you are the advisor to the king. You are wise beyond your years. I think we should go and lay eyes on this witch. I want to thank her for allowing her daughter to attempt this and for all the planning and effort they are making for those of us trapped in our kingdoms. I want to take one of my mother's jewels for the young witch to show our appreciation. Fetch me the royal jewels and we'll choose and then go see her.

I think that's a wonderful idea Sire. I'll return in a couple minutes.

Guard! Come here. I want you to go to the gate and tell the woman waiting there that I will be with her in just a few minutes. I have something to clear up before I can come, but ask her to please wait.

Yes Sire.

He was barely gone to deliver the message when Albert returned with a large jewelry trunk. Baltaazar opened it and began to take items out one at a time. I don't know what this girl looks like so I'm not sure what will complement her. He said as he continued to remove and peruse beautiful pieces of jewelry from the trunk. AH HA! I've found it. He lifted a stunning necklace from the box. It was a very large, pear shaped, sapphire in the deepest cleanest blue that had ever been found. It was hanging on a long gold chain. It would probably reach to her elbows. I've always admired this piece. It's simple elegance shows the beauty of the stone and enhances the beauty of the wearer.

Oh, Sire, she will love this. It's absolutely stunning. What a precious gift to bestow.

Put the rest of the jewelry back in the trunk, secure it in the safe and join me quickly so we can meet this white witch Miranda.

Miranda heard the footsteps of the two guards, the king and the other man with him as they approached the gate. She ventured a look inside and realized she was face to face with the king. She quickly dipped low into a perfect curtsey and awaited his command for her to rise.

Rise Miranda. I am pleased to meet you.

Your Highness she spoke as she nodded her greeting.

I am thrilled with your news. So thrilled I've

overcome my fear of meeting you. I wanted to thank you in person for what you and your daughter are going to attempt for us. I also want you to extend my thanks to everyone who's helping in any way. Is there anything we can do from here to help you?

No Sire. I even debated on whether to tell you about our plan, but I decided you needed some hope and joy in your lives; and you needed to be aware should anything go wrong. We truly don't expect anything bad to happen, but felt it my duty to warn you non-the-less.

We have what we'll need and as we're witches, we can manufacture anything we don't have, so the only thing I can think of is maybe have everyone stay inside the palace that day. Keep the courtyards empty. My only fear is that the sight of you or Angelica would fuel the fire in Zythora and possibly give her added strength born of revenge. I truly don't want anyone harmed and we're taking extra precautions in Drenidore with all the inhabitants as she will be so close to them. We're shielding them in the four corners of the realm before we start the spell.

I'm glad you're thinking it all through. I thank you for protecting my wonderful wife Angelica and the rest of our kingdoms. I have a gift for your daughter. It will help her focus on us during the battle. Please tell her how grateful I am. He handed her a blue satin pouch. Go ahead, take a look at what you're going to be taking her. Miranda opened the pouch and pulled out the necklace. She gasped, looked him in the eye and said.

Your Highness, this is too much. It is beautiful, but we are not asking for payment of any kind. This is all from our hearts, especially Cassandra's. We have been friends with Angelica and a wolf boy in the forest for some time now. His name is Javan. He is very helpful with anything we ask and he stands watch over Drenidore and Angelica as well. He is very devoted to her.

It's not payment, it's a gift from my heart. It was my mother's. I want her to have it and to wear it; especially during the battle. I hope it complements her.

Oh it does, her eyes are deep blue. Quite like yours and this sapphire.

Wonderful, then I chose wisely. I think it's why it was my mother's favorite gem to wear, it was like looking into my eyes. Tell her I will be honored to see her wearing it when we meet on her birthday next year after the battle.

I will Sire. If there is anything I can do for you between now and then, just send me word. We are staying with Queen Lorissa, in her palace. I will always be your servant Your Highness.

He smiled, nodded and acknowledged her deep curtsey. Until July

Until July Sire. She waited until he had turned before she moved to leave. It had gone well. He was pleased. He knew of their plans and he had sent Cassandra an amazing gift from his heart for his gratitude for the sacrifice she was making and the risks she was taking in order to break the curse and free everyone in the two kingdoms. It was a good day with an even greater day coming. Miranda walked down the street and turned into an alleyway before disappearing as she didn't want to cause a stir. She was home within the minute.

Cassandra! Come here please.

Mama, you're home! I've missed you.

I spoke to Baltazaar and he's very pleased with our plans and he sent you a gift to show his gratitude. She took the pouch and slowly pulled the necklace from the pouch.

Oh mama, this is beautiful! I can't believe he sent me something so precious. Can I wear it all the time, or is it just for special times?

We'll put a spell on it so you won't lose it. Tell me what kind of spell do we need to perform?

Well, I think we need to bind it to me so it can't come off. That way I won't lose it. Is that right?

Yes it is, we call that a binding spell even. Tell me what you think you have to speak.

Powers of earth, nature and sun
Grant to me powers this chore to be done
Bind to me this beautiful necklace of blue
But allow me to remove it when I want to
Does that make sense mama?

It does and you've done it.

What do you mean I've done it? I didn't do anything.

That's why I tell you that you must be careful every time you speak as your power is strong and just saying the words makes a spell work. It doesn't have to rhyme or be wordy. You are so strong you may not even have to invoke the powers to make it work. Let me show you it's working. She took hold of the necklace and lifted it as to remove it from her and she couldn't lift it high enough to take it over her head. You see, it's bound to you and no one can take if off except you and it cannot just fall off either.

Wow mama, I do need to be careful. That was very easy and I didn't even realize I'd done anything.

You can probably activate a spell if you just think it in your head. Like you made the food appear just by thinking about it. No spell was spoken, just the thoughts in your mind caused it to happen. It was created exactly like you thought it would be.

It's good you're that strong, you just need to be aware of your thoughts so your magic doesn't get away from you.

I'll do my best mama. I'd sure hate to harm someone by something I just thought about. I guess that's why everyone doesn't have magic. Could you imagine the damage those men in the tavern could do if they had magic. They are crazy when they're drinking. It's hard to think about what could go wrong. All things and people have a purpose and a way about them. I'm glad you instilled in me a loving heart. You are such a good mama.

They hugged and decided it was time for dinner when both their stomachs growled at the same time.

21 – The Final Year

It was a year of change, growth and preparing. They continued all their exercises to increase their strength and magic.

They spent even more time together to strengthen their bonds. Cassandra would fly on Greargon's back and not even have to pull on the reins for him to know where she wanted to go, how fast he should go, or when to stop. They were in tune, as they should be. It was in late August when he began to get his fire. They kept that a secret from Peter and Millie as he didn't want to be embarrassed should they see his first attempts. He and Cassandra would practice after they went home each day or before they arrived. They would stay near the cave and the pools of water inside, should he have an accident or not be able to control the direction or volume of fire he was expelling.

At first he was coughing smoke. Cassandra would come home smelling of smoke but she said nothing as she knew Greargon was changing as well. Soon he would feel the burn in his throat as though he'd eaten something spicy. During this phase, he wasn't coughing smoke, but he was very uncomfortable in that he felt like he was burning up from within. Then the fire grew stronger and stronger inside. He no longer coughed or sputtered, but he could feel it coming. He knew it was close and one morning he told Cassandra he was ready to try it. She stood by his side as he attempted breathing it for the first time. He basically coughed out a few flames in short bursts.

Don't be discouraged my friend. You must have patience. This is not automatic, but must be practiced and perfected. It's foreign to you and of course you will cough instead of breathe smoothly as your body is adjusting. Do not be discouraged, it will come; and when it does, you will amaze the world!

It was less than a month the he went from coughing smoke till he was breathing fire. It was small flames at first, then bursts of flames and then full on streams of fire. She was right by his side every step of the way. She watched as his designs illuminated on his chest and the undersides of his wings just before he breathed fire. She knew there had to be some sort of significance in the way they were designed. They were specific designs and she asked Miranda about them.

I know I said I want designs to appear as his fire built, but I didn't design any. I had no picture in my mind of what they should look like, so where did they come from mama, and what do they mean?

They came from you because you said you
wanted them, you just weren't specific so they
came from your subconscious. Can you show
me the designs?

They look like this. Cassandra drew the symbol
that appeared on Greargon's chest and the
one on the underside of his wings. This first one
is blue like his back and glows on the grey of his
chest. They really are quite beautiful and sort
of mesmerize you when you gaze upon them.
Maybe that's a distraction feature for your
enemies. I don't know, but I love them being
there.

The second one is under his wings on the teal
color. They too glow that same blue as his
body. Neither can be seen until lit by his fire. I
know I keep saying it, but it is truly a beautiful

sight mama.

I've seen both these symbols Cassandra, the one on his chest is for strength and resilience. The ones on his wings are the symbol for fire. It's almost like a warning if someone sees them glowing as he's flying over, they can rest assured he is about to breathe fire down upon them. Many times dragons will raise up on their two hind feet and spread their wings when they breathe fire, thus giving a warning again that you are about to be burned to a crisp. I hadn't thought about the symbols catching the enemy off guard, I'd always just thought it was a warning. Is he getting pretty good with his fire? Do you need any help with his training?

He is getting good with it, it's been a while developing from smoke to fire, but he's doing well with it. Thank you but we don't need help. We want to keep his fire a secret from everyone but you, and we don't want anyone to see it if they even think he can or find out he can. It's to be part of the scene during the battle with Zythora. I hope you don't mind mama.

It's fine dear, it will be a beautiful thing to witness and a fearful thing for Zythora. There are spells to protect from fire, and she's quick enough to invoke one, but if she's not expecting a dragon and he rears up ready to breathe fire, she may just not have enough time to stop it, no matter how fast she is. That's another reason we want him to be invisible. So she won't see him coming. Every single element of surprise we can have will only help our fight.

That's what we were hoping too.

After another six months of training he could breathe fire for an entire five minutes before he had to take another breath. He had perfected his aim and his depth perception was spot on. He could hit his target from one foot or one thousand feet away. Of course the closer he was, the more force there was from the fire. He was accurate during flight, from a standing position, sitting, or even lying down. He was most majestic though, when he was reared up, standing on his back feet with his wings spread.

Once he perfected the breathing part, he began working on spitting fire balls. It's the same intensity of heat, but they'll almost knock you down with the force of the blow when you're hit. They're usually bigger than the person is and the fire burns once you're staggering from the blow or knocked down from it. Should the witch put herself in a protective bubble, or behind a shield you can't burn her with the fire, but she also cannot send any magic your way. She can, however remove and replace the shield very quickly.

This is when the dragon would move in close and be holding his breath for as long as necessary to be at the ready to expel a ball or stream of fire.

Greargon had been working on his breathing as well. He had increased his blowing time from five minutes to seven, but he was really in need of a quick gasp at that limit. He could do forty fire balls before he needed another breath and he could hold his breath for twelve minutes anticipating the moment he could spit fire balls or breathe fire. This was pretty impressive and the opponent probably wouldn't think he could last that long.

When they weren't training, they were having fun. She, going to school or playing with Peter and Millie. Together, flying, playing games, reading, doing word puzzles. They both loved to learn. Chess had become one of their favorite games as it was a game of strategy.

Peter and Millie loved the pools that Miranda had put in the cave. They didn't know they were to extinguish fire if necessary. They thought they were for Greargon to drink from and for them to swim in. They would slide down his tail towards a pool and Greargon would lift it at the end to sort of toss them in. There was a great splash as they flew into the air and then hit the water.

They made regular trips to see Javan and Angelica to keep them apprised of their progress and just to spend time with their friends.

Javan had grown as well. He was no longer a young wolf, but full grown and very muscular as he ran a lot and used his muscles to push limbs and such out of the way as it encroached upon someone's house or fell on their pathways. He was committed to caring for the forest, and worked hard at keeping it safe to move about and live in. It would have been easier in his human form as he'd have hands to work with, but he made do and did his best. He was always helping someone or doing something to keep busy as the confinement was driving him crazy. He wanted to be free in the worst way.

They had gathered the town folk together a couple more times for dinners. They had another party for the whole town and this time Greargon was a bigger hit. They had become used to him and had seen him flying around a few times. He hadn't done any damage or harmed anyone so his line filled up fast as everyone wanted rides and they didn't just ride this time; they talked to him too. They were enthralled with his speech and his beauty. He was a commanding figure and extremely intelligent. He had read every book Miranda and Lorissa owned and it was quite an extensive library. It had high ceilings and was on the first floor, so he would go in there to read. He would curl up among the books and read for hours. It kept him busy when Cassandra was in school.

They had helped build new playground equipment for the school and some benches for the park. Peter, Millie, Cassandra and a few other children joined Ms. Catherine in making flower beds and planting them around the school house. It was so pretty once the men had given it a coat of paint.

Miranda had two more cooking parties during the year so they would have plenty to eat during the winter. They'd preserved meat, applies, berries, pears, sweet potatoes, and more. She'd given away more chickens, beef and hay. She had soap and perfume making days with Ms. Catherine and LaDonna. They had so much fun even though the work was hard.

They had established themselves in this town and everyone was pleased with the arrangement. It was easy to forget they were witches when they dug in and worked as hard as anyone else in the group. They were dirty, sweaty and tired, just like everyone else at the end of the day.

22 – The Battle

The day had arrived. Cassandra awoke with a sense of purpose she'd never felt before in her life. It was THE day. It would forever change her life. She would succeed or fail. Live a life of joy and happiness or die a horrible death or worse yet, be punished for all eternity at the hands of Zythora. She was good at punishing and with all that time trapped, she was like a festering boil, growing ever more ugly by the day. It had to be dealt with, but no one wanted to be near it for fear it would explode all over them. That was something that just might happen literally or figuratively today.

It was her birthday, but that thought never crossed her mind. All she thought about was it was the day she would go to battle with Zythora for her friends' freedom.

Cassandra stood looking into the mirror at the young lady staring back at her. The hair color was the same, the eyes and even the few freckles left on her nose, but this was not the girl that went to bed in this room last night. This girl was carrying the weight of the world on her shoulders. This girl was the only hope for thousands of people, animals, creatures, and kingdoms. This girl knew what she had to do and didn't regret it one minute because she'd trained for this for a little over three years and she believed deep in her heart that it was her destiny and she wanted it. She was hungry for the moment she would face Zythora as she'd seen the oppression of those under the curse. She'd seen the sadness and it had made her angry that they could all be so mistreated because they were bystanders to someone else's internal issues. She had eaten, breathed, and slept it for years and she had practiced, perfected, and focused on it all that time as well. Oh she'd had fun and friends, but she had been blooming, developing, and changing into this girl. This girl had so much power in her mind and hands. This girl was all grown up at the ripe old age of 16. This girl did not long to play games or run away from today. This girl was a warrior and she was trained, fit and mentally ready for this challenge. This girl was excited that this day had arrived and she could prove her statement three years ago that she knew in her heart she was the one.

The little girl was gone. This girl was strong and if she survived this day, she would be crowned queen of the white witches. Not just her coven would be subject to her, but all good witches would be. It was unthinkable what this girl could accomplish today. She looked down at the sapphire around her neck. A token for her to remember who she was doing this for, but she always knew. She was doing it for Airamoor and Drenidore, but more importantly she was doing it for her friends Angelica and Javan. The girl that went to bed still had a few doubts and concerns that maybe this would not be possible; but this girl knew better. She knew the final outcome of this day would be victory over evil. This girl knew it would be an exhausting day, but she didn't care. She was ready for the challenge. This girl was still sweet and kind inside, but nothing would stop the drive she had for vengeance this day. It was time for retribution and it would come at her hands.

Cassandra smiled into the mirror and softly said, Good-bye Cassandra. You've been a wonderful little girl and you've had the spirit to make this girl you see in the mirror what she is today. Queen Cassandra salutes you for your bravery, perseverance and love for this world and all its inhabitants.

She then turned and began to wash and dress. She was slow and methodical as she considered every aspect of her appearance and this day. She made herself a new outfit for today. It was pure white. It fit her loosely so it was comfortable to move in. It was simple like a young girl would wear, so as to fool the enemy. Her sapphire nearly glowed against the whiteness of it. She made some slippers to wear. They were a simple brown and were very comfortable. She braided her long golden strands so they would not fly into her eyes, but lay securely on her back. She lifted her wand and decreased its size to slip into her pocket.

When she was dressed, she looked around at her room and with a small wave of her hand transformed it into a woman's room. All dolls were in a box in the closet and her dresser was filled with jewelry, makeup, perfume, scarfs, belts and other accessories. She vowed she would return to this room today, but it would be the room of a young woman, not a little girl. It would age her as well so she would look more like a young woman too.

She headed to the kitchen where her mother was waiting. She immediately came and embraced her. I am not worried about you today my dear, but I am a little sorry that you have to grow up this way. You will be years more mature than your friends at the end of today and you won't be quite so carefree and playful as you were yesterday. Growing up is a big change, but you have it under control. It may bring the same change to Peter and Millie, but not in the same degree. I imagine it won't change your friendship, but everyone will look at you differently. They'll show you honor and respect, love and appreciation. They'll recognize the poise and grace with which you carry yourself. I'm sure you saw it yourself in your mirror this morning as you dressed. It shows in your choice of attire and how you exude confidence in yourself.

I said good-bye to little Cassandra. It wasn't as hard as I thought it would be. I like this girl that I've become. I like the confidence you have helped me attain. I like the wonder in the eyes of my friends when they look and me and think about what I'll be doing for them today, but I still see the love we've shared these past three years. We've been good friends to each other

I've made waffles with chocolate and strawberries for our breakfast this morning. I know it's one of your favorite meals. Then we'll talk about the rest of the day.

These are wonderful mama. Thank you. I do love this breakfast. I'm ready if you are.

I am dear and everyone else will be by now as well. So, one more time, here's the plan: Angelica was to have everyone to the corners by eight this morning. They've spent the last month digging holes deep enough and large enough for everyone to fit in. I will speak the protection spells and put them in bubbles in the holes and cover them with dirt. This should keep the magic from being sucked away and allowing Zythora to find them and do possible harm. I want to do as much of the preliminary stuff as possible to conserve all your energy for the battle.

Next step will be to raise Zythora's box from underground and remove the bubble from her and her box. You'll have to do that as that spell is tied to you. We'll keep her bound in the box so she'll still be secured, but it will allow the forest to drain her energy due to her very own spell dispelling all magic inside the borders of the forest. That will take a few hours but it will not drain all her power.

While we wait, the white witches from everywhere will gather in the field by our house. We have a couple thousand here and are expecting another five hundred or so by noon. When we are ready to begin, they will begin chanting in a tight circle around you and then as the powers build, they will begin to step back and open the circle up until they are surrounding you on three sides and are near the perimeter of the field. The power will continue to flow, but you will have room to move and Greargon will have room to maneuver into position. Nothing and no one will be between you and Drenidore. After that all the white witches will speak the spell together to release Zythora from her bonds and then we wait for Zythora to release her spell.

The very second she releases Drenidore from the curse so that she may exit, we'll attack. If we don't give her much time to assess the situation, we can catch her a little off guard and we'll gain the advantage early on. We don't want her to be able to replace the spell before we attack. This way their magic will be restored and they may be of help.

You'll speak the spell to destroy her powers and body and as you begin, Greargon will attack her with his fiery breath so she's busy with him while you cast your spell. Once spoken, we'll all join in and repeat it three times. Greargon will continue with the fire until she is destroyed.

Fire is the only natural thing that can destroy a witch. Magic is the only supernatural thing that can destroy a witch and we'll have both hitting her at the same time.

That covers everything I believe. When do you want to start?

It's almost 8:30 so let's begin at 8:31 even time will be chanting for us as the clocks hands will be moving up instead of down.

Miranda sent the mental message while Cassandra went outside to greet Greargon.

Greargon had just finished checking himself, doing some breathing exercises and admiring his figure in the reflection of the pond. He was just as sure of this day as Cassandra was and truly he was itching to get it going so it would be over and done with. He had worried about this long enough. They were all prepared and there was no way they couldn't prevail.

Good morning Greargon. She said as she came close to him. He bowed his head and she laid hers on his nose and reached up to stroke his jaw. You are magnificent. I knew you would be ready for this day. You are fully grown and stand thirty six feet tall. You are an incredible sight to behold when you are standing and a fierce opponent when in flight. As no one has seen your fire yet, I am sure jaws will drop and opinions will rise as they see you strike fear into any who would even begin to consider opposing you. Your strength and beauty are beyond compare. I am so glad you are mine and we have such love between us. Are you ready my friend?

I thank you so much Cassandra. You are quite the figure to behold yourself. There is more to you today than yesterday. You also will be a fierce opponent and a winning one today; of that I am sure. I will be at your side and obedient to your command. I want everyone to be happy and free to live their lives with joy and love. I cannot imagine not being able to love you or feel your love. I am ready.

We know the plan, it's been set for months now and mama just went over it with me again so I am ready as well. Don't forget Zythora will have a say in how it all goes, but hopefully we'll stay one move ahead of her and all will be well. Come, let's get this show moving.

They emerged from the cave like the battle had already been won. They looked confident and triumphant, but they did have a little trepidation in their hearts, not enough to want to back out, but enough to be careful.

They were met by Miranda and the town folk. Everyone cheered and whooped and hollered for them. Miranda and Cassandra mounted Greargon and off they went, waving to the people as they disappeared.

It was less than two minutes before they landed in the field outside Drenidore. Greargon needed to stretch so he flew very fast to limber himself.

The minute they dismounted they performed the first steps in the plan. The residents of Drenidore were safe in their bubbles, thanks to Miranda. Zythora had been raised from the ground, but kept in her box, thanks to Lorissa's spell. Her power was being drained, but she was so powerful it wouldn't have a great effect on her, but it could be just enough to make a difference in the battle.

They waited there four hours and then all the white witches came and surrounded them and Lorissa spoke.

It is time sisters. "Chant sisters, chant for the powers of goodness to overcome the powers of darkness then after twenty repetitions, we'll speak the spell to release her from her bonds. So they began to chant:
Powers that be, give us the power
Powers of light, expel the darkness
Powers that be, give us the power
Powers of light, expel the darkness.

As they chanted over and over in unison, they could feel the charge of power surge through them. They felt the energy flow through the entire group. Then they all spoke the spell to release Zythora from her bonds.

They felt her move. So they began to chant again. When they felt the power flowing to Cassandra, they slowly began to move away from her and Greargon to the perimeter. Cassandra lifted a protective barrier that would keep them from being seen by Zythora. When Greargon attacked, she would remove the shield and they could cast the spell to destroy her. They never stopped chanting as they were waiting for Zythora to make her move. They had to be ready. This was their chance to free the world.

Greargon moved to the left side of Drenidore, just in front of the forest. He nodded to Cassandra and made himself invisible. He didn't want Zythora to see him until he was ready and in position to fight her. If he could wait until she was several feet into the field, then he would attack from behind her while Cassandra and the witches attacked from the front. Cassandra stood alone in the middle of the field staring straight ahead, watching for Zythora. She was alert and at the ready, the instant she came out of the forest, they would attack.

Zythora pushed with her magic and the box splintered away from her. She arose and looked around. She reached out with her magic. She could not feel a single living creature. This was odd. Maybe it was because she was weakened due to the curse on Drenidore. It was draining her of her magic, she could feel it trickling away. It was slow, but it was a power loss none the less. She wasn't worried yet as she still had lots of power at her disposal and she needed to check things out. She looked all around. She was definitely still in Drenidore, but she was alone. This made no sense. Surely they all wouldn't have died. Maybe someone found a way for them to leave, but had they broken that part of the spell, then surely they would have broken the entire curse and she would not be feeling the drain of her powers.

She found a puddle of water and looked at herself. Yes, she was just as beautiful as the day they'd imprisoned her. Well, there was no use lingering here. Everything she wanted was in Airamoor so she had to see if she was able to leave Drenidore. She was in the middle so no side was closer, so she walked toward Airamoor as that's where she was headed anyway.

She was searching with her mind and magic to find someone, anyone, but there was no one there. Maybe the curse was shielding them from her. She pushed harder with her mind, seeking outside the forest. She still could not feel anyone, but she did feel the tingle of magic. Was it the curse causing that? It seemed so faint. She wasn't sure, but she kept walking. When she reached the edge of the forest she looked out in every direction and all she could see was the house in the field. She stood there for several minutes watching, searching, reaching out for someone or something. When she decided she was alone, she removed the curse and Drenidore was opened up and she stepped forward. The light flooded back inside the forest and immediately life came back to it. Plants started growing and flowers too long in darkness opened their blooms and soaked in the warmth of the sun.

Cassandra dropped the barrier and spoke the spell to remove all her powers and make her mortal again. Greargon attacked her with fire balls, knocking her forward towards the center where Cassandra lifted her wand from her pocket high into the air and began to speak the spell for the second time and was joined by all the covens. She was drained drastically every time the spell was repeated. She finally managed to cast a spell for protection and strength, but it was too late, they had become so powerful working as one unit that her spells were useless against them. Cassandra pointed the wand directly at Zythora's heart and spoke the spell the third time as Greargon was still attacking with streams of fire. The magic pierced her heart before she had time to respond. This brought her down and her protection was gone. They repeated it a fourth time and she was mortal. There was no magic left in her.

Cassandra! What say ye? Do I fry this former witch or let her die naturally?

Zythora screamed out not to be burned and Cassandra had mercy on her. If you could call it mercy. She was about to receive the worst curse ever to be uttered in history.

She banished her to a cave in the great mountain not to be visited, not to be loved, never to gain any magical powers and to age a thousand years every earth year until she died of old age; ragged and alone in her cave with only her conscience to keep her company. Her beauty would fade with the first day and she would come to despise herself. Her only protection was from herself. No matter what she did, she could not kill herself. She could inflict harm, but would not die from it. She was doomed to less than a year in all reality; watching herself wither away knowing she'd lost everything and those she'd cursed so many years ago would live long healthy happy lives together. It was enough to drive her crazy before old age ever destroyed her.

With a final flick of her wand, Cassandra sent Zythora to that cave. Never to be heard from again.

Everyone was exhausted, but not too tired to cheer loudly and shout their praises and thanks to Cassandra and Greargon.

They released the residents of Drenidore from their protective bubbles and everyone came pouring out of the forest into the sunshine that they'd longed for so many years. They were whooping and shouting thanks and praises to the powers that be. They were hugging and then everyone stopped suddenly. There it was love. They had felt the stirrings of love again. Wives and husbands embraced, children received hugs and kisses. Even the trolls were smiling and slapping others on the back and laughing with each other.

Angelica asked Greargon if he would wisk her to Airamoor so she could deliver the good news. Cassandra nodded and off they flew.

Baltazaar was walking out of the castle with tears in his eyes. He had felt the surge of love enter his heart and knew Zythora had been defeated. He looked up just in time to see Angelica slide down Greargon's leg. They ran to each other and embraced as the people began pouring from the castle with love and joy in their hearts once again.

Back in the field, a young boy was embracing Cassandra and declared his love for her.

Javan, I think I have loved you from the first day we met.

I can't say I loved you then because I couldn't feel love, but I grew very fond of you over the years and then today, there it was. The moment I could feel it, I did.

Cassandra! Miranda called out as she ran

toward her. You did it. I'm so proud of you. I love you so much. And what's this? She asked as she reached them and they had finally pulled apart.

It's love Miranda; and I do love your daughter so much. I know a lot about her, but I want to know more. Is it ok if I join you both at Lorissa's castle? I hope we can explore the things we each like and decide if this is a love that will last or a moment in time brought about by extraordinary events. I don't want to rush anything as we need to be sure, but I so want the chance to find out.

If it's ok with Cassandra, it's fine with me. I've noted what fine character you have and how devoted you've been since we've met. You've done everything we've asked and more. You've been supportive and attentive to your queen and your kingdom. I think you'll make a fine husband when you're both ready.

Cassandra! We need to talk a minute while everyone is gathered here.

Of course Lorissa, whatever you need, I'm here.

I don't need anything dear, I want to give you something; and I truly want it to be today. I propose we and our sisters transport every single being in this field to my castle along with

all those inhabiting Airamoor and we'll have a
great feast and a coronation for our new
queen. Are you up for it today?

Absolutely and what a celebration it will be.
Everyone will be happy and free. Let's do it.

Lorissa made the announcement and in less
than ten minutes, everyone from both
kingdoms and all the witches and Greargon
were at Lorissa's castle. A stage was set, tents
were up with tables and tables full of food.
Musicians were playing and decorations and
flowers were everywhere.

It took just a few minutes for everyone to settle
down and then the ceremony began.

Cassandra had made herself a new gown for
the occasion. It was silver with thousands of
sapphires attached all over it. Her gift from
Baltazaar was hanging around her neck, resting
elegantly just inches below her neckline. Her
hair was braided up and there was never a
more regal woman seen. She was a vision and
when she walked out on the stage, a hush fell
over everyone. Her beauty had literally
brought them to a standstill and had left them
mesmerized. She was stunning and she was
their queen.

Lorissa began speaking and telling everyone

the story of their champion and the incredible journey she had undertaken to ready herself. It truly was a joint effort between all of them. They trained, planned and dedicated themselves. They came to this battle as one and because of that, they succeeded. After 650 years, Zythora's followers and sister witches, had given up on her returning; thus leaving her to battle alone. Being trapped in her own curse didn't help her either. The curse on Drenidore began draining her powers the minute she was released from the bubble. She explained they all owed their lives to Cassandra; and even though she would from this day forward be Queen of All White Witches, she was truly supreme ruler of both their kingdoms. She was also their protector and guardian. Baltazaar and Angelica would rule Airamoor and Angelica's brother Hunter would rule Drenidore. His coronation would take place as soon as Angelica could make arrangements.

I now crown thee Queen Cassandra and she placed a beautiful crown of sapphires and pearls onto her head and everyone cheered.

Now we also have another to honor today. Please cheer for Greargon.

Once the cheering had stopped she continued. Greargon, I want to honor you as

Keeper of the Realm. You are truly wise, honest and a great protector. You never once waivered, or thought of yourself. Your concern was the safety of the people and inhabitants of the kingdoms. You are a great and noble dragon and will be revered by everyone forever. You are charged with protecting our new queen and remaining her obedient servant and right hand. Thank you for all you have done for us all. She extended her arms up and in her hands was a sapphire encrusted emblem with the fire symbol on it. He bowed low and she put it around his neck.

I am truly honored as I have the utmost respect for you Queen Lorissa and you Queen Cassandra.

There were more cheers and then Cassandra stepped forward.

First of all, I want to thank you all and I promise to be the best queen I possibly can. I do have a first item of business as queen. While Queen Angelica and my mother, Miranda, have been there every step of the way, they both had very personal reasons for their love and support, but there is one who served from their heart and devotion to their kingdom. We have one more to thank and honor here today and that is Javan of Drenidore. I do wish to acknowledge he is to receive your respect and honor for all he did to help us in our quest. I also wish to acknowledge he is now courting the Queen and our new journey is beginning today.

And they all lived happily ever after, or did they?

Thanks so much, I hope you enjoyed.

I would appreciate you leaving a review on any or all of these sites: **Amazon.com, Goodreads.com or Author Kathy Roberts on Facebook**

Your feedback will help me improve as well as help others determine if they'd enjoy this book.

You might also enjoy my other books:
"Scars of the Heart" and **"Truth Heals the Heart"** (a duology, but both are stand-alone books as well). These novels were set in medieval times, with lots of mystery, murder, kidnapping, espionage, treason and of course romance.

"The Elevator" a paranormal book where Samantha is trapped in an elevator by something or someone until she can free 500 souls and find someone to take her place.

"Chasing the Rift" Sci-Fi about time travel set in my home state of West Virginia.

"Adventures With Freddy" My 6-book, children's full color self-help/teaching series is being released in 2017-2018 Subtitles are: "I Can Scare Monsters", "Where Do My Vegetables go?", "Watch Out For The Toy Snatcher!", "I Want to Stay Up!", "I'm Not Afraid of the Dark!" and "Who's Afraid of the Storm? Not Me!"

All my books can be purchased on Amazon.com in paperback or e-book. I also sell from my website if you'd like autographed copies.
Https://www.authorkathyroberts.weebly.com